Spinner's Mystic Travels
Lost in the Black Forest

by

H. L. Perry

To ERIC
Best Wishes
12-25-03

DORRANCE PUBLISHING CO., INC.
PITTSBURGH, PENNSYLVANIA 15222

ISBN # 0-8059-6291-3
Printed in the United States of America

First Printing

For information or to order additional books, please write:
Dorrance Publishing Co., Inc.
701 Smithfield Street
Third Floor
Pittsburgh, Pennsylvania 15222
U.S.A.
1-800-788-7654
Or visit our web site and on-line catalog at
www.dorrancepublishing.com

I would like to thank my parents, John and Kay Crabill; my husband, Jimmie; my children, Chris and Donna; and my sister, Wendy, for their constant love and support.

Contents

Introduction

This is the story about the adventures of a lazy, likeable, slightly over-weight spider named Spinner. Spinner, as the story is told, learns a lot about what he can (and wants to) do to protect his friend, Tump, when both are lost in the forest together, and try to return to their home, Witches' Brew. As a result of his adventures, he learns to be more empathetic toward his fellow creatures, making him a more positive creature.

Spinner has a lot of stories to tell and we are hoping that he will come to have a captive audience. Also, the author has illustrations within the story line that make Spinner's adventures with his friends come to life throughout the pages.

Chapter One

Out in the middle of nowhere was a forest known as Witches' Brew, where a fat spider named Spinner lived with his family and friends. On a sunny day in mid August, Spinner was lazily lying on his web soaking in the sun. A gentle breeze was swinging him back and forth. As Spinner was enjoying the solitude, along came his friend, a stinkbug called Harley, who hadn't seen Spinner in a long, long time.

"Spinner, where have you been? I have been all over the forest, looking for you!" Harley's eyes welled up with tears as he approaches Spinner.

Spinner looked up at Harley and smiled, "I haven't been home for very long. I just need to rest today and soak up the sun." Spinner got up, stretched his legs, and moved off his web.

Harley gasped as Spinner sat down beside him. "What happened to your legs, Spinner? It looks like two of them are missing!"

"One and a half actually, I still have part of this one." Spinner turned to Harley.

"What happened Spinner? No one knew where you were, including your family. We have all been so worried about you," Harley said as he roughly hugged him.

Harley was expecting Spinner to push him away, but he didn't. Spinner even hugged him a little tighter. He loved Spinner, even though he was mean to him most of the time. But as he moved back and looked at Spinner's face he could see that something about him had changed. It seemed to come from within. He seemed wiser and more caring. Harley knew that he had a gift. He could see through to the real heart of creatures. Although some seemed mean and even

1

cruel, Harley always knew if that was the way they really were, or if it was just a put-on. Harley also knew inside, very deep inside, that Spinner was a very caring creature. Spinner didn't show it often, but it was there, just waiting to come out.

Harley could tell that something big had happened to change Spinner while he was away, and he wouldn't leave until he heard his story.

Harley looked over at his good friend, "Okay Spinner, tell me, what has happened to you?"

"I will tell you what I can, but you may find it unbelievable and hard to understand once I begin, so bear with me if I can't share it all with you today. It also involves our old friend, Tump," Spinner started to explain.

"Do you remember the day when I was so frustrated and mad because Jo Bob, the hummingbird, flew out of nowhere at amazing speed and dove into my web? What a mess he made of it! And he was laughing as he flew away. Anyway, I ended up telling you that I was going to go ballooning. As you know, being a spider has some advantages. I don't need a whole web to fly from tree to tree. I can explore using the wind to take me for a ride with just long pieces of the web." Spinner continued, "Well, shortly after I had made this decision, Miles called to me from the tree."

Spinner began to tell Harley exactly what had happened to him.

Chapter Two

"Spinner, come here. I need to talk to you," whispered Miles from the tree.

"I really don't have time, I need to get out of here for a while. What do you want?

"I'm not in the best mood today," I growled.

"Yeah, I saw the number that Jo Bob did on your web. Listen, Spinner, I am in tune with the mystic forces of the deep woods. The signs are all bad. You should stay home today." Miles's voice sounded so eerie.

"Why should I listen to you? I have no idea what you are—or if you really are a friend!" I retorted.

"Now Spinner, have I ever given you bad advice? Or harmed you in any way? Just because you can't see me doesn't make me an enemy. Evil is afoot. Stay home, fix your web, and have a snack," Miles said.

As I walked away I did think about what he had said for a fleeting moment, but then dismissed it from my mind. It was a beautiful day and I was determined to enjoy it ballooning above the trees. The forest looked so breathtaking from above. The trees were deep green and the sky was the color of a robin's egg. I was wishing that I could stay up forever. Well, I could if the wind would let me.

Just then a down draft of air grabbed me and I went falling to the earth extremely fast. I went crashing through the trees; I tried to grab a branch or leaf to break my fall, but I just kept falling. I landed on the spongy ground with a bounce. It was much darker on the ground. It smelled of pine needles and mushrooms. Well there I was, lost and alone. It was me and my superior wits against the forest…no problem.

Chapter Three

As I started to walk through the forest, I ran into my old friend, Tump. Tump is a trapdoor spider. A trapdoor spider catches his prey without a web. He uses camouflage to hide and jumps out of his hole to catch his prey. Tump had taken a leaf and covered it with mud. He jumped up at me as I walked by.

"Gotcha!" Tump yelled as he tried to pull me into his hole.

Of course I weighed a little more than Tump, so he couldn't pull me in.

"Wait, Tump, it's me, Spinner. Quit drooling all over me!" I spat.

"Spinner? What are you doing here?" said Tump.

Tump hadn't changed much since I had last seen him. Then I realized that it had been a long time since I'd seen him. His black hair was short and stuck straight up. When it came right down to it, he wasn't very smart. But he had a kind soul, and I truly liked him.

"Hi, Tump, long time, no see. How have you been?"

"I'm doing fine, what are you doing here? Awfully far from home, aren't you?" asked Tump.

"Yeah, I had a slight problem with the wind. Where am I, Tump?" I asked.

"You are in the forest, standing by me," answered Tump.

"I know that I'm in the forest, and I know that I'm standing next to you! I want to know *where* in the forest I am!" I yelled.

Tump pondered my question. All at once his face lit up. "You are at the north end of Witches' Brew Forest, as far north as you can go. The mountains are through the trees over there." Tump pointed toward the tall pine trees to my left.

5

Oh boy, I'm farther than I thought. The wind was blowing the wrong way, so no ballooning home for me. The trees were so thick that I couldn't tell what time of day it was. But my stomach told me that it was way past breakfast.

"Hey Tump, do you have any food around?" I asked him.

"No, I ate a slug this morning, but nothing since then," he answered.

"Well, I need to find something to eat." I was getting very hungry. As I started to leave, Tump asked, "Can I walk with you for a while?"

"Sure, Tump, come on," I said.

As we walked through the forest, I heard strange noises. I heard a hiss and jumped.

"What's wrong Spinner? It's just a snake. Snakes don't eat spiders," Tump said smiling. He talked the whole time we walked. I should have left him behind, but if I couldn't find any food, he could be a snack. The mushrooms were huge around here. They were orange-tan and had a musty aroma, I wondered if I could eat one. On top of one of the mushrooms was a bright green grasshopper.

"Hey, man," the grasshopper said, "you're on my lawn. Walk somewhere else."

His eyes were red and one of his antennas was broken. "Hey, didn't you hear me? OFF THE GRASS!" The grasshopper yelled.

"My, Tump, isn't he awfully rude?" I asked, with a big smile on my face.

"Yes, he is. We should teach him some manners," said Tump.

After we ate our rude snack, we started to walk again. Tump told me that I would have to go through the deepest darkest part of the woods to get home. He called it the Black Forest of the woods. Tump said that a lot of his friends had gone into the Black Forest never to be seen again. I was willing to bet that they went in there to get away from him. I was getting bored hanging out with Tump. I decided that I would let him take me to the entrance, but no farther. He told me I would have to cross the Troll Bridge. Guess what lived under the bridge—a troll, of course.

We walked for what seemed like hours not saying much. I didn't realize that the forest I lived on the edge of was so vast. The trees seemed to get thicker and thicker. The path was slowly disappearing. The forest was so different here. There were monarch butterflies and moths of every color. In my family we don't eat butterflies or moths. We also leave ladybugs alone. We eat the pests of the world.

There was nothing of beauty to be seen here. The air was heavy and damp. Even the trees were ugly, moss hung heavily from the branches. I neither saw nor heard any birds. As we walked, I could feel things moving under the damp leaves. How could Tump like living in this part of the forest? I needed to feel the sun on my back. When and if I got out of here I'd never complain about my home again.

"How did you get here to start with?" I asked.

"Well," Tump said. "I was walking across a branch on that big dead oak tree near your web when I slipped. I fell and fell, then plop. I landed on the back of a bird. The bird flew for hours, then he made a sharp left turn and I lost my grip. I fell off and kept falling until I hit a leaf on a tree and then landed on a mushroom. When I landed, a gray dust covered my body; it came out of the mushroom. I got up and looked at myself in a puddle. I screamed. I saw a ghost. So I ran and ran. And every time I looked in a puddle there was the ghost again. So I'd run some more. Then, after an hour of running and looking at puddles to see if the ghost was still following me, I noticed something. The ghost looked awfully familiar. Do you know why Spinner?" Tump asked.

How can Tump be so dense? I thought.

"No, Tump, I don't know why. Please tell me the rest of your story."

"Well, Spinner, it wasn't a ghost at all. It was *me* covered in mushroom spores! Wasn't that funny? Tee hee hee! I was running for nothing! After that I just stopped, dug a hole, and made my home, right there where you found me."

"Don't you miss your family?" I asked. "Don't you want to go home?"

"Yes," Tump said with tears in his eyes. "But I'm too scared to enter the Black Forest to get there."

I knew that I couldn't leave Tump there, no matter how much he annoyed me.

"Tump, we are going home together. I won't let you stay here alone."

Tump looked at me with fear in his eyes. "Nooooooo…I can't go with you. Not in there, not there through the scariest part of the forest."

"Now listen, Tump, did it ever occur to you that the reason you never heard from your friends again is because they made it? I'm sure that they didn't die. They made it to our side of the forest and didn't want to come back here," I reasoned.

Tump stopped, deep in thought. "I never considered that." At last a smile came to Tump's face. "Okay, Spinner, I'll go with you. But I'm still scared. Even though I know you won't let anything bad happen to me."

So we picked up our pace and walked down the narrowing path. What had I done? Now Tump was my responsibility. I didn't need this added pressure. The fact was, I was scared, too. I did believe the scary stories that Tump had told me. Since I am a big mean spider, not too much scares me. I can be as vicious as a snake and as cunning as a fox. We would be fine. As we walked, I decided to put my mind to good use. I thought of ways to catch Jo Bob. I'd get that rotten bird for what he had done to my web!

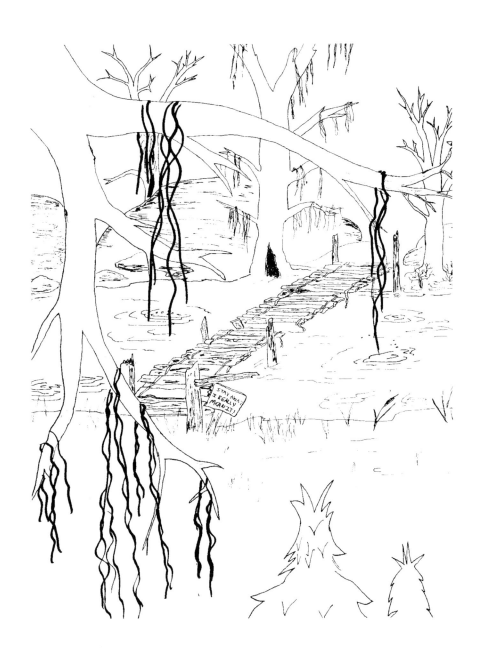

Chapter Four

I bumped right into Tump as he had stopped in his tracks. He pointed straight ahead. There it was, the entrance to the forest. We were staring at the Troll Bridge he had told me about.

Nothing about this place was normal. The trees seemed to reach down, instead of reaching for the sun. The bridge didn't extend over water. Instead, black and green goo surrounded it. The goo bubbled and burped. Nothing could live in there. At least I hoped not. A mist was creeping around us, and if we didn't hurry across the bridge, we wouldn't be able to find it. The bridge itself was old and rickety. It was gray and brown and covered with moss. The bridge was made out of sticks tied together with some kind of brownish green rope. A sign was nailed to a small dead tree next to the bridge. The sign said, STAY AWAY!!! I REALLY MEAN IT!!! All of the letters were painted in red. At least I hoped it was paint! There weren't any trees living close to the black goo under the bridge. Somehow the trees had managed to spread their branches across the gooey mess and meet the trees' branches on the other side. So, even with the wide expanse of the goo, you still couldn't see the sky. My heart sank; what had I gotten Tump and I into? This place made our starting point look like a fresh garden in the spring. Tump stood next to me, shaking. I hoped he couldn't read. Tump looked up at me and asked what the sign said. At least one thing was going my way.

"Well, Tump, it says, 'Welcome, please watch your step.'"

"Really?" Tump asked. "That's so nice of the trolls to care. I sure wouldn't want to fall in that mess underneath."

I walked up and down the bank and surveyed the other side. I didn't think it was possible, but the other side looked even worse.

Most of the trees on the other side were dead. Animal bones covere with moss and black mold littered the ground. I couldn't see anything past the dead trees. All was dark beyond them.

I turned around to see where Tump was. The mist was creeping ever closer. I was now or never.

"Okay, Tump, let's go," I said.

Tump jumped up and walked over to my right side. We walked to the foot of the bridge. I gingerly stepped up on it and tested my weight. It seemed sturdy enough. My heart was hammering in my chest and I was afraid if I talked he'd hear the fear in my voice. So I motioned for Tump to follow me. Slowly we walked, the bridge creaked and moaned as we went. The bubbling goo hissed and popped. Air bubbles popped on the surface. It stank, even worse than a stinkbug did. It smelled like rotten bird eggs that never hatched. Tump was right behind me, shaking as we went. He didn't speak, and I felt his hot breath on my back. Half way across I looked back and saw the thick mist licking the bank.

On we went slowly, carefully watching where we placed our feet. All of a sudden *crack*! Tump was falling through! He screamed, frantically grabbing with his legs trying to get a hold on anything. But the stick planks were slimy and he kept slipping.

"HELP ME, SPINNER!" Tump was starting to fall.

That black evil-looking goo seemed to be reaching for him! I quickly grabbed the rails with all eight of my legs. I shot out a stream of web. It latched onto Tump. I held on and pulled with all my might. The web became taut; I prayed that it wouldn't break.

"Hold on, Tump; don't wiggle around! I've got you in my web!"

Poor Tump was terrified; he was just inches from slimy, black death. Tump kept squirming around, yelling my name, and I was losing my grip.

"TUMP! DON'T MOVE! I HAVE YOU!" Finally he realized that he wasn't falling any farther and he relaxed. I tugged and pulled at Tump. He was now able to grab the stick planks of the bridge floor and pull himself up.

We sat down on the bridge to rest for a minute. Tump was breathing hard; he started pulling my web off himself.

"Are you okay, Tump?" I asked shakily.

"Yeah, Spinner, I am now. You saved me. You didn't have to. But you did and I'll be forever grateful." Tump was crying again.

As a spider, I hate all this emotional stuff. "Listen, Tump, you'd have done the same for me."

"Yes, that is true," Tump said, "I sure would. If I could be smart enough to think that fast."

As we rested on the bridge, the smell rising up from that black goo was making me sick. Tump had finally calmed down. We needed to leave soon. I couldn't believe how close I had come to losing Tump. This journey to get home was going to be long and dangerous. I knew that I'd have to keep my head. Our lives depended on it. The wind was whistling through the trees. Then I heard something else, a low, moaning sound. It was hard to make out what I was really hearing. How can I describe it? The sound was underneath the wind. The sound was being carried from very far away. The moaning sent cold chills down my back. How did I get into this mess? I wanted to go home. I wanted to see the sun again. I missed my friends and my tree. *Stop feeling sorry for yourself*, I thought. Time to move on, we sure couldn't stay there.

"Come on, Tump, let's get going. We need to get across this bridge."

We were walking gingerly across the bridge, gauging our steps carefully. I could see the end of the bridge up ahead. Tump had finally started talking again. He told me about all the strange creatures he had seen in the part of the forest he had landed in.

"You know, Spinner, this place is so different from home. I saw red worms three feet long. They had green eyes that glowed in the dark. And they hissed like snakes as they slid across the ground. Some days I wouldn't come out of my hole at all. Some fish have two heads and they fight each other. Can you imagine being hooked to someone you constantly fight with? There were other horrible sounds that I heard, but I was too afraid to peek out of my home and look," Tump said with a sheepish look on his face.

I hoped that he had just been seeing things, but I doubted it. This was like another world, a land that hadn't changed in a million years. How Tump had survived alone was a miracle.

"Look Tump, we've just about made it. There is the end of the bridge." Tump looked up at me and smiled.

I had missed that smile, so I was glad he was recovering from his fall. But then his smile faded away and was replaced with a look of sheer terror. I snapped my head around, scanning the bank. Then I saw it, a troll. It was twice my size and had kind of a human shape.

Well, you know, two arms and legs, one head. But that is where the similarity ended. It was covered in coarse gray hair, but underneath you could see green-gray skin. It was dressed in rags of various dingy colors, and he carried some kind of sharp weapon, maybe a spear, in his hand. Oh what horrible hands he had. They were all twisted and deformed. His knuckles were large and knotty. He had long yellow fingernails that seemed very sharp, and dangerous. He had a long beard and wore an elfin hat.

"What are thee doing on this bridge of mine?" he yelled. "Didn't thee read my sign?" He pointed. And then yelled again. "Thee both need to go back to the land thee belongs in." Tump started to cry, which made the troll laugh, a sickly high-pitched laugh. "Thee must go or meet thine's end. And a terrible end it will be!" Then the troll laughed harder.

Tump started to back up. I turned around and grabbed him. I was mad. I'd had enough. My heart was pounding hard. I was seeing red! *If that stupid little troll thinks he is going to stop us from getting home, he is wrong.*

I told Tump, "Now you do as I say. Remember, Tump, you are strong and can do this."

Tump finally looked away from the troll and looked at me. "But he'll kill us, we have no choice but to turn around and go back," he stammered.

"No, Tump, that smelly troll has no idea who he is dealing with. Have you forgotten all you used to hear about me? I've done all of those mean, nasty things and more."

Tump swallowed hard and said, "You're not going to eat me, are you, Spinner?"

"Of course not, Tump, you are my friend," I answered.

"Now, Tump, turn around and make the meanest face that you can."

If we weren't in a life and death situation, I would have laughed. Tump screwed up his face and what emerged was hilarious. But it was pretty scary looking, too. He looked like he had just swallowed an old ant egg and it had not agreed with him. Oh well, what could I expect? Tump had a kind face, not an evil one. Now I, on the other hand, could scare my mother. Which I actually had done, but only when the occasion called for it.

"Okay, Tump, follow me and don't say a word. Growl if you can sound convincing enough." As we walked forward, I had the most vicious-looking smile.

THE TROLL

"I told thee to leave the way thee came! Now thee will pay!" said the troll. As we approached him the nasty little smile on the troll's face disappeared. "What kind of monsters are thee?" The troll stammered.

"I am Spinner the Horrible, you've never heard of me? Now it's your turn to die! Like a vampire, spiders kill indiscriminately. But in your case I'll make an exception." A crazy laugh escaped my throat.

And then I charged the troll. Poor Tump tried his best to growl. I have to give him credit; he stayed right behind me, never hesitating. Well, that dirty little troll took off running toward the bank. I was right behind him, trying my best to grab him. He jumped right into the putrid water and somehow managed to swim to the other side. He emerged from the black goo screaming words at me that I never heard before, shaking his long skinny arms at us.

"Thee, just wait! I'll get both of you!! I'm going to the elders and they'll send our armies after both of thee!" the troll screamed at me.

"You go do that, troll. Spinner the Horrible will be waiting for you!" I laughed.

I turned to Tump, who was still growling, and motioned for him to follow me.

The troll had disappeared into the mist. I looked around. This place was dismal. All the trees that I could see were dead or dying. The ground was hard and littered with stones. The wind had picked up and I was getting cold.

Chapter Five

We walked past the dead trees and back into the forest. It was warmer in there. The trees blocked out the wind. It was also quiet, a little too quiet. The pine trees were tall, so tall that you couldn't see their tops. The floor was littered with dead pine needles. We found a nice-sized hole in the stump of a tree. So we brought in some pine needles and made a bed. Tump caught some slugs for us to eat.

"Go ahead and try them," Tump said. "They're not that bad."

I grimaced and ate one. Well, it could have been worse, we could have been the troll's lunch. Tump fell asleep inside the stump, snoring occasionally. But I couldn't sleep. I needed a plan. No, I needed a map. I had no idea how far we had gone or in which direction. I decided to climb the tallest tree I could find, so that I could figure out which way we needed to go. I found the perfect tree not too far from Tump and started climbing. I couldn't hear any birds. It was weird in the forest without birds chirping. It wasn't that I liked birds—they did their best to find and eat spiders. That was nature's law. There wasn't any reason to take it personally. When you are near the bottom of the food chain you tend to gain a little wisdom about these things. Well, at least I didn't have to worry about birds swooping down for a little spider snack while I climbed to the top. The farther I climbed, the more the wind picked up. I decided to tether myself to the tree as I climbed. I'd hook the web to the tree and go so far, release it and start over with a new piece of web. After about an hour I reached the top. Nothing looked familiar. I didn't recognize anything! As far as I could see, there was nothing but trees.

Then I spotted what looked like water, far off to my right. It was gray and shimmering. It had to be the lake my great-grandfather had told me about. It had to be the lake that all of the animals had fled to during the famine of 1937. But it was pretty far away. Tump and I had a long journey ahead of us. I spun down the tree on my web and took a nap with Tump beside me.

TEEKI

Chapter Six

We woke up an hour later feeling refreshed and ready to go. That slug really was filling. I wasn't the least bit hungry, which is a new feeling for me. I didn't want to tell Tump, but I was worried that a troll army might actually come after us. I figured we had just a few hours of light left, so it was time to get moving. The plant life on this side of the bridge was dramatically different. Not much of anything could grow through all the pine needles on the ground. There were some huge yellow-green plants with skinny pointed leaves everywhere, but no animal life. As far as I could tell, there were no other spiders around either.

About an hour into our walk, I noticed movement out of the corner of my eye. Tump stopped at about the same time and looked in the same direction.

"Did you see that, Spinner?" Tump asked.

"Yes, now be quiet so I can listen," I answered.

It sounded like chirping. *Oh no, could it be a bird?* I saw the leaves on one of those yellow-green plants move to one side. Red eyes peered out at us. Tump was shaking in fear, as usual. I leaped forward right into the center of the bush. It was getting dark, so seeing inside this bush was impossible. I felt around with my legs and grabbed hold of something. Whatever it was it was strong and squirmed around something terrible. When I had a good grip on it, I started backing up. Out in the dim light I was able to get a good look at my squirmy prey. I couldn't believe my eyes. It was fluffy like a baby chick, but what covered it wasn't exactly feathers or fur. It was something in between. It was the color of the sky at sunset, a red orange. Its eyes were buried in the wispy fur. I assumed there was a mouth in there somewhere. Its legs were long and skinny and gray in color. As far as I could tell, it had no arms. But it had a long tail with humps running down the center of it.

I sat down with this unusual creature and loosened my grip on it. It relaxed a little and started chirping again. Tump was like a kid with a new toy, or me with a fat tick. He touched the fur on its back and it started to purr.

Tump started talking to it. "Hey little guy, what's your name? Where do you live? How old are you?"

"Now, Tump, you don't even know if it can talk," I said more to myself than him.

"Of course I can talk; I'm a Teeki, what are you?" the little guy chirped.

I opened my hand and he jumped and then landed on top of Tump's head.

"My name is Teeki and I live here. I don't know where I came from originally. I eat plants, any kind of plant, nut, or berry. I've been following you for a while. What are your names?"

I answered, "My name is Spinner and this is my friend, Tump."

"Nice to meet you. I've never seen you around here before. Do you live here, too?" Teeki asked.

"No, we're not from around here, I'm afraid we are lost. We are trying to get to the Great Silver Lake. Have you heard of it?" I asked hopefully.

"No, I'm sorry, I've never seen a silver lake anywhere around here. We've always lived around here, and believe me, if there is a silver lake around, I would know," Teeki chirped.

"Teeki, I know that there isn't a lake in this part of the forest. But have you at least heard of it?" I asked impatiently.

Teeki sat on Tump's head with his legs crossed. "Yes, now that you mention it, I believe I have heard of it. My grandfather Orb used to talk about the Calm Sea that he had visited as a child. You see, before the trolls invaded the forest, my family used to travel everywhere through the forest. During the winter we would head south, where the plants would still be blooming. Where the plants were plentiful, that is where we would go. But now it is too dangerous. So we stay here, where the pine trees always stay green. And food is everywhere, maybe not the best to eat, but it will do."

"Trolls, huh! I ran one off by the bridge. That smelly little creep didn't scare me! By the time I was through with him, he was crying. They aren't as mean as they seem. Believe me," I laughed.

Teeki's face twisted up, his eyes got as huge as saucers and he jumped up. "Oh no, Spinner, you are wrong! They have killed more of my friends than I care to remember. They are strong together as a group. Spinner, they are relentless. Once they spot their prey, trolls don't quit until they have caught it. They will track you day and night. They are tireless and ruthless. If you did as you said and humiliated one of them, they will come after you. Oh Spinner, you are in trouble, big, big trouble!"

Now it was Tump's turn to cry, just what I needed.

"Listen, Teeki, I can handle those trolls, just tell me how your grandfather got to the Calm Sea. If those trolls are after us we have to get going, for our sake as well as yours," I said.

"You have to go through the misty bog," Teeki replied. "But you must be careful. There is quicksand. My grandfather also told me that it was haunted by all that never made it out of the bog. Do you see the heavy mist way over there? That leads the way to the bog. Stay on the path, don't wander off of it and you'll be fine. The path is the safest route through the bog. But Spinner, it is very dangerous, so please be careful."

"I hate to leave you now, Teeki. I'm afraid that the trolls will get you or your family if we stay here," I said.

"Don't worry about me, I'll stay high up in the trees. The trolls can't climb trees. I'll be fine, Spinner, you and Tump are the ones that I'm worried about. You'd better get going. Goodbye, Spinner, See you, Tump!"

With that Teeki jumped off Tump's head onto a branch. Up the tree he jumped from one branch to another. I couldn't believe how nimble and quick he was. Tump waved at Teeki and said his goodbyes.

Tump and I were on our own again.

Chapter Seven

"Come on, Tump, let's get moving."

What next, now that we had a band of extremely angry trolls after us? What little light filtered through the trees was slowly fading, but we decided to press on. We came to the path and the mist circled around us. It had a slight glow to it, which helped us see. We heard strange sounds all around us. I didn't like being out in the open like that, but I was determined to stay on the path as Teeki had suggested. Tump didn't talk and was constantly stepping on my heels. I didn't slow down our pace because I knew we were being watched.

I could also hear movement in the forest around us. As a spider, I have great vision. But looking into the forest was like trying to see through tar. I'm sure the moon was out, but it was no help. Not a single moonbeam could filter through the mass of tall pine trees that surrounded us. Walking on this misty, damp path, I was willing to admit to myself that, yes, I am a fat, lazy spider. But with unknown danger all around me, my strength increased and I was super alert. I moved along that path fast. But Tump was winding down. I constantly had to stop and wait for him. He was starting to breathe hard, so I began to hunt for a safe place to bed down for the night. Now I could easily climb a tree and make a web, and be fairly safe for the night. Tump was a trapdoor spider. He lived his whole life on the ground. Tump also admitted to me that he was afraid of heights, so I would have to find a place on the ground that was safe. Not an easy task in these woods.

"Hey Tump, I'm getting tired. Do you want to stop for the night?" I asked.

"Sure, that is, if you think it's okay. I'm real tired too," Tump said with a sheepish grin.

"Okay Tump, I want you to dig a hole big enough for both of us, just like the home you had when I first saw you, right over there in the soft dirt next to the path."

"Okay!" Tump said in a giddy voice. "I'll show you how good I can build a home, Spinner!"

Tump started to dig, and in no time he had dug a hole that would be big enough for both of us. He found a big leaf and started throwing some mud on it. I knew Tump was tired, but he worked hard and fast. I figured that he was trying to impress me. Until now I had handled everything, now he had a chance to help, too. I could tell that it lifted his spirits a little. I decided from now on, no matter how damp the earth was, I would let Tump provide the sleeping quarters for us.

Tump did an excellent job. The hole was lined with pine needles and was quite cozy. After Tump and I jumped into our temporary home, he pulled a mud covered leaf over it, and we were set for the night. Tump fell asleep almost instantly, but I couldn't. I had too much on my mind. This bog didn't seem very inviting. I wasn't as worried about the quicksand, but what about the ghosts? How do you fight a ghost? I had no idea.

I had just slipped off into a light sleep when I heard a branch break. I snapped fully awake. The sound wasn't from overhead; it was from the forest floor. And whatever broke it wasn't small. The first thing I thought was; *it must be a human*. Now I had heard the horrible stories about little kids pulling the legs off spiders. It made me shake just thinking about it. I had seen poor wingless flies wandering around in such pain. Needless to say I tried to avoid the places humans were known to visit. *Crack*, another branch broke. Whatever it was, it was getting closer. Tump had dug the hole pretty deep, so I knew a human foot wouldn't crush us. Then I heard a roaring sound. Tump woke up with a start. He had a calm look on his face, which threw me for a loop.

"Dragons don't eat spiders."

"Dragons! You've got to be kidding!" I shouted.

"No," Tump said, "I've seen them before. One night I couldn't sleep and went for a walk and I saw them. The dragons only come out at night. They hunt for night wings. That's what they eat, you know," Tump said in a matter-of-fact voice.

"Night wings?" I asked, "what are night wings?"

"They look kind of like a black bird, only they don't have feathers. Now *they* do eat spiders and any other insect they can find." Tump shivered. "They are scary."

I heard another roar, but it was further away.

"What do dragons look like, Tump?"

"Well, they're not as big as you would think. If I would have to guess, I'd say they were about four feet long. Their bodies are gray-green, and they have scales. Their wings are dark gray," Tump said.

"Wings? You mean they can fly?" I asked.

"Yea, but not real high. Just a little bit higher than the trees." Tump yawned and went back to sleep.

Dragons, I thought. *What next?*

I woke up early in the morning. Tump apparently had been up for quite a while. He stood next to me grinning, holding two slugs. "Thank you, Tump, what a nice breakfast."

We ate quickly and headed down the path once again. Daylight didn't help the look of this place much. The mist was still clinging to everything, giving it a scary, dismal look. Spanish moss seemed to be hanging on every branch available. Old pinecones littered the forest floor. The mist was cold and damp. I didn't think I'd ever be warm again. We picked up our pace once again; if the trolls were back there, I planned on keeping ahead of them.

We had been walking for quite a while and making pretty good progress. The bog couldn't be much further. The path that we were on had widened quite a bit. I had decided that tonight when it started to get dark, we would quit walking for the night. I didn't want to meet up with any of those night wings.

Two hours later we reached the bog. As far as I could see there was water. Not the clear water I was used to. This water was murky green with patches of brown scattered here and there. I could see that in some places the water was very shallow or there was no water at all. I guessed this was what they called a bog. It reminded me of the place where we bury our dead. We lay them to rest on a leaf and then push them into the sacred water. The green muck sucks them down, never to be seen again. My hope of getting across the bog quickly and safely was dashed. I had planned on jumping from tree to tree using my web. But the trees were spaced too far apart for my plan to work. Tump was looking at the bog, but he stayed away from the edge. I thought I could make out a path weaving crookedly through the bog.

"Well, Tump, we've made it this far, so let's go a little farther. What do you say?" I tried to sound upbeat about the whole thing.

"Sure, Spinner, I'm with you one hundred percent!" Tump said with a smile.

The mist was even thicker in the bog. I had found a long stick and was poking it into the marshy ground. I planned to avoid the quicksand at all costs. It was slow going, but I felt safer in this thick mist. We were invisible to anything more than twelve inches away from us. But it also made the path hard to see. Several times we had to backtrack because the path would disappear. I heard things moving around in the water. I hoped it was something normal that belonged here.

The path twisted and turned left then right. There were huge cattails sticking up everywhere. The reeds were bigger than any I had ever seen, but there were pretty blue flowers scattered around. They looked like violets but were bigger. This bog looked prehistoric, everything was three times its normal size, and in a way, everything looked dangerous. Even the flowers looked as if they were ready to reach out and bite us. The mist had distorted everything; it was like looking through a bubble. When I looked up, no sky was visible. We were being smothered in a gray mist. Even breathing was hard. I couldn't hear anything. I thought of the time that I had gotten my head stuck in a knothole overnight. It had taken forever to get out, but this was worse.

The path made its way to the edge of the water. I didn't like that one bit. Who knew what was lurking right under the surface? But there wasn't any choice in the matter. If I wandered off the path, we would never make it out alive. Tump was right behind me; he had also found a stick and was gingerly poking it into the ground. I didn't bother telling Tump that I had already walked on the ground he was now poking. If it kept him occupied and unafraid, that was fine with me.

The green water had lily pads three feet wide. Small yellow flowers sprouted from them. You could see algae underneath. I noticed some ripples in the water, and before I could react, a huge crocodile surfaced inches from us. Tump yelled and dropped his stick. We both backed up, but we really didn't have anywhere to go.

"Well, two spiders; I haven't seen a spider in years," the crocodile boomed in a low, mellow voice. "Why do you two look so scared? I won't eat you, both of you are too small." He looked directly at me. "But I must say, you are the fattest spider I have ever seen. And I'm old, I just had my three-hundred-year birthday."

"I beg to differ," I growled. "I'm not fat, just a little short."

"So you do talk," said the croc. "What are your names? My name is Gulp."

"I am Spinner and this is my friend Tump. Nice to meet you."

"What are you doing here? This isn't the safest place for two small spiders," said the croc.

"We are trying to find the Calm Sea, on the other side of the forest. Have you heard of it?" I asked.

"Humm, yes I have, but it is very far away. Much too far for two little spiders to travel. There are many dangers in these woods," Gulp said.

"I know that," I said impatiently. "We've been chased by a troll."

Gulp looked up. "You've had a run-in with trolls?"

"Yes, and he still could be after us," I said.

Gulp continued, "Trolls are bad news. I hate them; they terrorize the little creatures of the forest. I'd eat every one of them, if they didn't give me such a stomachache. If the trolls come this way, I'll do my best to stop them. You are almost halfway through the bog, but you will need to stay alert. The worst is still ahead of you. Watch your step, Spinner, and stay on the path. If you make it out of here, you'll come out at the foot of Black Mountain. You will have to climb it; there is no way around. Beware of the caves; don't go in any of them. If you do, you'll never be able to find your way out."

I called to Tump, "Let's get going."

We thanked Gulp for all his help and advice and off we went. I felt a little better knowing that Gulp would be on the lookout for the trolls. I was getting hungry; it must have been close to noon. Tump found an anthill, and we ate way too much. I really wanted a nap, but we pressed on. The path veered away from the water, and reeds were surrounding us.

"What did you say, Tump? Speak up, I can't hear you," I said.

"I didn't say anything Spinner, I wasn't even humming," Tump said.

"Well, don't you hear that? The whispering? They're saying my name," I asked angrily. "Where are those voices coming from?"

"Spinnnnnerrr commme here. Weeee want tooo talk tooo youuu-uu…Spinnnnerrr…"

"I heard it!" Tump said, "where is it coming from?"

"I think that it's all around us!" I answered.

"That's impossible, it can't be all around us," I said, "we would see something."

"N-n-not if they are ghosts," Tump stammered.

"Come out," I screamed, "come out where I can see you!"

The air around us had cooled off in the last few seconds. Even though I couldn't see it, I could feel movement around me. Tump tried to run, but I grabbed a hold of him.

"Tump!" I yelled, "if you run off you'll get lost. If they are ghosts, they can't hurt us. They're all dead, remember? Let's keep walking, maybe they will go away."

"But why are they here?" Tump asked.

"Well, maybe spirits can get lost in this mist like living creatures," I answered.

We slowly started to walk, being careful to stay on the path. Up ahead I could see a huge oak tree. It must have been three hundred years old. The base of the tree was easily five feet across. There were knotholes the size of saucers all over it. The voices were beckoning me to come closer and closer to the tree. It seemed to me that the rest of the world had disappeared, all I heard were the voices, and I knew I had to go to them.

The tree was well off the path, but I was powerless, I had to look at the tree. Off the path I stepped, getting closer and closer to the tree. The sweet voices were calling me, it sounded almost like a song. I could barely hear Tump. What was he saying? Oh well, it didn't matter. The voices grew stronger and stronger. I walked even closer, but then I stopped. Not because I wanted to; I was stuck, for some reason my legs wouldn't move. Then the singing stopped, and a horrible laughter replaced the song. What had I done! Where was Tump? I hoped that he hadn't followed me. I was sinking in quicksand. Oh what had I done, why didn't I take the same advice I had given Tump? The more I struggled, the faster I sank. My only hope was Tump—he had to help me.

I looked around and there was Tump, waving his arms frantically.

"Spinner," Tump screamed, "why don't you hear me? Answer me, please!"

"Tump!" I yelled, "I hear you, now I need your help. I'm sinking, find some way to pull me out."

Tump took off to find something. I was sinking fast, and I didn't hold out much hope that Tump would get me out in time. Poor Tump, he'd be left alone in this horrible place. And I'm going to die here, far from home. I wondered if anybody would even miss me.

I was almost covered when Tump came to the rescue. He had found a long branch and dropped it across the quicksand. He bravely crawled across the branch. I got a hold of Tump and pulled myself up. He hugged me, crying all the while. When I caught my breath, we crawled across the branch to safety.

"Thank you, Tump, you saved me," I said in a shaky voice. "I don't know what came over me. I felt like I was in a dream. I'm sorry, Tump, I didn't mean to scare you. I let down my guard; it won't happen again, Tump, I promise."

I was scared. It seemed like the ghosts had taken control of me. I didn't ever want to go through that again. It was like being a puppet, and whatever was pulling the strings had a nasty sense of humor. Gulp had told us it would take a lot longer to travel through the rest of the bog. That meant we would be sleeping here at least one night, maybe two. How could we protect ourselves from ghosts? The only thing to do was to get as far from this spot as possible. There weren't any ghosts when we had entered the bog.

"Are you ready to go Tump?" I asked.

"Yes, I don't like it here. Let's get going," Tump said.

As we passed a big oak tree, I could hear the angry voices screaming at me. They sounded frantic and so sad. If Tump heard them, he showed no sign of it. I blocked the screams out of my mind but couldn't help wondering how they died. Those poor lost souls sounded like they were in so much pain. Maybe I should go back and help…*STOP IT SPINNER!* I screamed in my mind. They were trying to draw me back, into the quicksand.

"Talk to me, Tump, I need to hear your voice," I said.

"Okay, Spinner, do you know what I'm going to do when I get home?"

"What, Tump?" I asked.

He answered, "I'm going to give my mom a big hug. You know," Tump said with a shaky voice, "I almost forgot what her voice sounds like. I wonder if they still live under that big elm tree? Do you think they will remember me?"

"Yes, they do, Tump. And I know they will be very happy to see you," I added.

Tump was smiling as he said, "I miss them so much. When we get home it would be so much fun to have a party. We could invite all of our friends and family to welcome us back."

His face was beaming at the thought of being home again.

Chapter Eight

I was getting so tired. That place was so dismal. I couldn't understand how anything could live there. I knew that if I didn't get home soon, I'd just give up. I missed my home and my family. I even missed Jo Bob, as mean as he was. But I couldn't give up, now that I had Tump to take care of, and I didn't want to let him down. I know that I am probably one of the meanest spiders around. That is my nature. If I was sad every time I killed my lunch, I'd never eat. While it is true I have a bad disposition, I can't stand ignorance. Well actually, I can't stand much of anything. But I knew my responsibilities, and somehow I would get Tump home. Nothing would stop me, and if some creature tried to hurt Tump, it would have to get through me first. And I could guarantee that it wouldn't be pleasant.

The ground was mushy and cold. I didn't think I'd ever be warm again. I smelled a combination of rotten wood and mold. I was beginning to wonder if anything, including us, could make it out of here alive. And what about this path? I had no idea if it actually led out of the bog. What if it was leading us in circles? That thought terrified me.

We stopped at another anthill for supper. The ants were plump and juicy. After such a filling meal, we decided to rest for a while. Finally, we forced ourselves to get back on the path.

After an hour of walking, the fog started to get extremely thick. It was cold and damp and clung to me like my skin.

"Tump!" I yelled, "hold on to me or I'll lose you." In the fog my voice wouldn't carry. The sound stopped as it came out of my mouth. "Tump, do you hear me? Answer me Tump!" I groped around trying to find him. All that I came up with were handfuls of air. "Tump!" I screamed, "where are you?" I turned around and headed back the way I came. The only way that I could tell I was on the path was by feeling along with my feet. "Tump! Please answer me," I prayed.

But I heard nothing but my own breathing. I had to stop and collect my wits. When was the last time I knew for sure that Tump was behind me? It was at least ten minutes ago. I was so deep in thought that I didn't even notice he was gone. A horrible sadness washed over me, and tears rolled down my cheeks. I felt my way back down the path yelling out Tump's name as I went. I knew it was futile. My voice sounded like a whisper. I prayed that the night wings hadn't gotten him. But if they did, wouldn't I have heard him scream? Maybe not in this blasted fog.

Night was quickly descending on me as I hunted for Tump. I had been hunting for over an hour, and the tiny spark of anger in me had turned into a red, hot flame. If something had taken Tump, it would pay dearly. It would pay with its life! I was crawling on the ground at this point, hoping to find Tump's tracks, when I noticed trampled grass to the right of the path. Instinct told me that this was the way Tump went, or was taken. But if I got off the path, I knew I would be lost forever, so I started a piece of web at the edge of the path and spun it as I walked. The trail of bent and broken grass was easy to follow, even in the fog. I found a clump of hair stuck on a thorn bush. I knew it had to be Tump's. My spirits were raised a little. At least I was heading in the right direction.

I didn't believe it was possible, but it was even scarier off the path. All the plants had one form of thorn or another. They poked and scratched me as I went. The rotted trees' branches seemed to be reaching for me, with gray twisted fingers. I heard a faint rustling in the trees and picked up my pace. The ground was black and charred. It had blue-gray moss growing all over it. Poor Tump, he must be terrified.

All at once, a blast of air hit me. It was pitch black, so I couldn't see what had caused it. I spun around peering into the darkness. *Whoosh!* I felt it again. I threw myself to the ground, but it was too late. Searing pain coursed through my back and I was lifted off the ground. It had to be a night wing! I could hear wings flapping up and down. I needed to think of something fast. I would either be eaten or die when I plummeted to earth. Its leathery wings flapped against the tar-black sky. Up and up we went. I managed to squirm around, even though it caused considerable pain. Claws dug deep into me. Just as my grandfather had been, I was blessed with large pointy fangs. So I opened my mouth and bit down as hard as I could. The creature let out a squawk and its talons opened. I took that opportunity to wiggle loose. The night wing tried to grab a hold of me again, its claws barely missed me.

Well now I'd really gotten into a mess. I was plummeting to the ground at a terrific speed, and it was pitch dark, so I couldn't see where I was falling to. In those few intense seconds, I thought of the family and friends that I would never see again. *Crash*, I hit the top of a tree. The branches cut and battered me as I plummeted through it. I must have blacked out when I hit bottom, which was probably a good thing. I'm sure I wouldn't want to remember the landing. When I came to, I was bleeding and bruised. Every inch of me hurt, but I was alive, and for that I was thankful.

I started to get up and screamed in pain. I felt along my leg, gently pushing here and there. It was worse than I thought. My leg was broken. Now what was I going to do? I sat there and sobbed, not only from the pain, but also from the desperation of my situation. Tump could be dead for all I knew; if not, I knew that he was in deep trouble. And what could I do now? I was broken and battered, body and soul. *Oh, Tump, where are you? I need your help badly.*

I pulled myself over by some big leaves and covered up in them. I sure wouldn't last through another attack from a night wing. As I looked down at myself, I couldn't believe what I saw. My web was still intact! I could follow it back to the place where I was attacked. Maybe I'd find Tump yet. I'd wait out the night and try again in the morning. I knew that I wouldn't be able to follow my web in the dark, and in the morning I would be able to see the extent of my injuries. As I lay under the leaf in the darkness, I realized how close I had become to Tump. I was thinking about the fact that he wasn't just my responsibility, he was my friend and I was sorely missing him. Without Tump lying beside me, I realized just how cold the bog got. In the darkness I kept saying silent prayers for Tump and myself. The light of day couldn't come soon enough for me.

Chapter Nine

In the morning I felt the few shafts of sunlight that had managed to filter through the trees. The light warmed my body. I surveyed the damage to myself. It was bad. My leg was twisted in a horrible way, and was bleeding. My back and shoulders were stinging, and when I reached around I could feel deep gashes the night wing's claws had inflicted. I wasn't even hungry—that was bad. I found two straight twigs and laid them on either side of my broken leg. I used my web, which is quite strong, and bound them around my leg. The tighter I tied it, the more it hurt. But I knew that I had to straighten out my leg. The pain almost made me pass out, but then I thought of Tump. I had to be strong for him.

I found a larger stick not too far from me on the ground to use as a crutch. I gingerly stood up and tested my leg with the crutch. The pain was bad, but I was tough. As I lumbered along, I realized how grateful I was that night wings only came out after dark. I followed my web, praying that it hadn't broken somewhere along my flight. As I moved, my broken leg bones ground together. Three hours later, I found the crushed trail I had been following the night before. I decided not to yell for Tump. I didn't want to alert his captors I was near. I had no idea how I would rescue Tump. I was in bad shape and they would have the advantage over me.

The trail opened into a clearing and there was Tump. He was tied to a rotted stump crying his eyes out. The clearing consisted of several dead trees. The grass around them was brown. Moss hung heavily from the gray branches. His captor was a cross between a scorpion and a worm. It was a weird shade of purple and blue. It had coarse, red hairlike spikes all over. The barblike spike on the creature's tail really worried me, too. It was long and black and was dripping with what looked like venom. It looked like a scorpion but moved like a worm. The only advantage that I had was that it would move more slowly than me. Tump was still alive, which was a miracle, but I didn't think it would be for long. There was saliva dripping from the mouth of the *scorpworm*. It definitely looked hungry. As it moved along, it made a slurping, sucking sound that turned my stomach.

I moved around to get closer to Tump, careful to stay out of sight. I hid behind a dead berry bush, trying to get Tump's attention.

"Tump!" I whispered, "Tump, over here!" Tump shakily turned his head, looking around. His face lit up when he spied me.

"Spinner!" he yelled.

"Shhhhhhh, be quiet, Tump. I'm going to help you, but please do as I say."

The scorpworm turned our way, and I ducked down behind the bush.

"Who are you talking to? No one can help you now. Your friend will never find you, and guess what? If he does show up, I'll have you for breakfast and your fat friend for lunch," spat the scorpworm.

Tump put on his bravest face and told the scorpworm that he would never allow that to happen.

"Ha, your time is up, and what can you possibly do to help your friend? One prick from my stinger and you are dead," sneered the scorpworm.

Tump's lip started to quiver, but he didn't cry. I was really proud of him; not too many spiders would have been that brave in his situation.

Anger had gotten the best of me. I was in a rage. *No one* treated my friend like that. I didn't care how big that thing was, and it was three times my size, it was going down. I threw down my crutch and stomped into the clearing. I was livid, and gratefully, I didn't even feel the pain in my leg.

I screamed at the scorpworm, "Soooo, you think that you are going to eat me and my friend."

As I circled around it, I tensed up, and then jumped on it. I started hitting at it with my legs. I sunk my teeth deep into its throat. The scorpworm squealed and tried to push away from me, but I knew that if I let him go he would get me with his stinger. He had fangs and they sank deeply into my shoulder. A burning fire started to spread through my back, but I didn't let go. I bit him again and the worm fell over. I was on top of him and had the advantage. My considerable weight helped me pin him down. The fight was far from over. I didn't have a lot of strength, but my anger made up for it. The scorpworm brought its stinger around and lunged at me, almost striking me. It spit green goo in my eyes, temporarily blinding me, but I held on tight. He started to wrap his body around me and squeeze me. I couldn't breathe, and if I didn't act quickly, I'd soon pass out. I punched with all my might, and my hand sunk deep into its body. The scorpworm screamed and turned to the left. My vision was starting to clear, but my eyes were watering and burning. It finally loosened its grip on me. I had hurt the creature, but not enough. It growled and spit at me as I bit it again.

Tump was screaming at the top of his lungs, but I didn't have time to worry about him. This was a life-or-death battle, the worst I'd ever been in. I stuck my hand deeper into his body and finally found what I was looking for. I wrapped my hand around the pulsing muscle and pulled with all my might. Out came the heart. It was still beating. I threw it down in disgust and hoped there was only one. Finally, the scorpworm went limp and I was able to roll it off me. I lay there trying to catch my breath and saying a prayer of thanks. When my breathing finally slowed down, I sat up.

"Spinner!" Tump yelled, "Are you okay? I was afraid that you were dead. Can't you talk? Oh please answer me," Tump begged.

"I'm fine, Tump," I lied. "Just give me a minute to catch my breath."

As I rested I took inventory of myself, and the injuries were extensive. The splint was gone and my leg was twisted beyond recognition. I was cut and bruised. When the scorpworm bit me, it must have injected some kind of venom. It was making me sick all over. Now instead of just my shoulder burning, my whole body did. My vision was blurry. My fever was worse. I had no idea how I was going to make it across the clearing, much less out of the bog. I wanted to lie down and sleep, but I knew that was the last thing I should do.

I had to get to Tump and untie him, so that he could help me. Slowly, I crawled over to Tump and let him loose. Tump hugged me crying all the while. I didn't say anything to him, but his hug was excruciating. Poor Tump was trembling as he let go.

"Oh, Spinner, I thought he was going to kill you. I don't know what I would have done if something had happened to you. You are my best friend, and I love you. I know that I'm a burden, but I'm going to do my best to pull my weight. I promise that I'll never get caught again."

"Listen Tump, I'm hurt really badly, and I'll need your help. My leg is broken, I'm running a fever, I've been poisoned, and I'm in shock. I'm afraid I'll pass out, so you need to find a place where we can hide and I can rest."

Tump looked at me, and his eyes widened. "Spinner, it's all my fault," Tump sniveled. "You're going to die, aren't you?"

"No, if you help me I'll be just fine, right as rain." But I wasn't at all sure how I was going to do. I knew that I was badly hurt.

Tump gently picked me up and we started following my web. We made it back to the path much quicker than I thought we would. Tump was strong. He wasn't even winded. He carried me to the edge of the path and laid me down carefully. Then Tump dug a hole and put a thick layer of pine needles on the floor. He gently laid me in the hole. It felt soft and warm. Tump told me he'd be right back and pulled a leaf over the hole. I was dizzy and sick to my stomach, but somehow I did manage to fall asleep. Later on, Tump emerged from the forest with sticks to make a splint and some water. He had used the top of an acorn to hold the water. He was much more resourceful than I had thought.

He sat down beside me and held the acorn to my mouth. I drank the water greedily and started to choke. Coughing hurt my back and sides, but I thanked him for his help. I showed him how to set and splint my leg. I screamed as Tump moved my leg and straightened it. The pain traveled all the way up my leg. I was thankful that Tump was quick, and had my leg set in no time. I then fell into a sound sleep. I don't know how long I slept, but when I woke up Tump had found some food. I thanked him for the meal, but told him that I wasn't very hungry. Tump's face dropped, which made me feel badly.

"I'll take some more water, if you have some."

Tump jumped up and returned with the water. I drank the cool water while he ate his meal.

I was pretty sure that I wouldn't live to see tomorrow. I could feel the poison from the scorpworm working its way through my body. I was already weak from the fall, so any chance my body had to fight off the poison was slim. Cramps racked my stomach continuously and I knew I had a fever. If we could just make it over the mountain, Tump could probably find his way home from there. Maybe sleep would help me, at least that was my thought as I drifted off.

The pain was just as intense when I woke up. The nausea hadn't stopped. The fever was blazing away and on top of everything else I was stiff. My leg was numb, so at least that was good news. Tump had been up for a while and had found breakfast. I couldn't stand to see the disappointment on his face again, so I choked down a little food. My throat was sore and dry so I drank the water slowly.

I knew that if we stayed here much longer, I would never leave, so I told Tump to get ready. Since it was late in the morning, the fog was lifting. I saw that Tump had found another makeshift crutch and had leaned it in the hole next to me. It took a lot of effort to climb out of our temporary home. I was very shaky when I walked, but I kept moving forward very slowly. Tump noticed my progress and put his arm under mine to help me.

"I'm so sorry that you got hurt. If I was smarter this never would have happened. It would have been better if you had never met me," Tump said sadly.

"No, Tump, it could have just as easily happened to me. And you are not stupid. You have to be intelligent to last as long as you have in the woods on your own for all these years. Please don't put yourself down, I don't like that. I need your help now, so quit feeling sorry for yourself. I'm hurt, Tump, I'm hurt badly. I have to depend on you now, but I have faith in you. I know that you will come through for me," I said.

We didn't talk for a long time. I was doing my best to keep from screaming, so words were out of the question. I started to notice that we were in a different part of the bog now. Even though it was dismal, there was still beauty. Purple and yellow flowers sprung up through the pine needles. Dew beaded in the leaves and looked like diamonds. The air smelled of pine, and in the morning air, it smelled so fresh. I had to figure out how to prepare Tump for his journey home, which he would probably make alone. Tump was stronger than he thought.

Deep in thought, I hadn't realized how far we had gone. "Tump, let's stop for a few minutes."

My leg was throbbing. Everything was swimming around me and I was sweating profusely. Tump helped me down onto the mushy ground. I had hoped we would be out of the bog by now. My injuries had slowed us down. At this point, Tump was practically carrying me. He never complained or slowed his pace. He knew that he had to get me out of here as soon as possible. We rested for about ten minutes and then started off again. I was in and out of consciousness. I was see-ing wild visions, flowers with eyes, talking trees, and pink balls of light. I know that I was babbling nonsense. I could see concern in Tump's eyes, but I couldn't stop myself.

We trudged on the rest of the day. I looked down and noticed that Tump was wading through ankle-deep water. I was so sick of this bog. Surely we would be out of it soon.

I knew that I had found a real friend. I was getting ready to tell him something, but it drifted out of my mind. My leg was totally numb, now I couldn't even move it. My heart was hammering in my chest. I didn't know how much more my body could take. The venom that the scorpworm had injected into me was definitely doing its job. I couldn't take deep breaths anymore, which terrified me. Tump was carrying me as gently as he could, but every bump jarred me painful-ly. I refused to scream. I knew Tump was doing the right thing. He had to get me out of there. The dampness in the bog wasn't helping my soreness. I was hot and cold intermittently, sweating one minute and shivering the next. Some hero I turned out to be. I couldn't even save myself.

Our lunchtime had come and gone. Even though I couldn't pos-sibly eat anything, I told Tump to stop. He came back with two slugs and pleaded with me to eat one. The thought of food made me sick. Tump apologized for bringing the food and eating it in front of me.

I told him, "No Tump, it's not your fault. Please, you go ahead and eat. Maybe I'll be able to eat later." The cramps in my stomach were unbearable. Pain shot through me like lightning. I rested while Tump ate and must have dozed off.

Chapter Ten

In my dream, I was at home, talking to Miles. He was telling me to rest, and that I would make it out of the bog. But that was stupid. I was home, not in a smelly bog. He wasn't making any sense, but what was new? He was always talking about something crazy. His voice had a no-nonsense sound.

"What's wrong with you, Miles?" I asked. "Are you mad at me? You're usually in such a good mood. Why do you sound so dire? We're fine, it's a sunny day and I'm feeling good. Don't look so sad."

"No, Spinner, everything isn't fine. This is a dream, and you are badly hurt. You need medicine and rest. But the potion is hard to make, and you don't have the strength to gather the herbs you need to make it. It is very important that you get out of the bog. The trolls are after you, and catching up quickly. You must wake up and go. It isn't much farther and you and Tump will be out. Once you are out of the bog you can hide, without worrying about getting lost," Miles said.

I had not noticed Miles's eyes before. They had a silver glow. It was almost hypnotizing. But could Miles be telling the truth? I was feeling great, better than normal. But was I? This did seem like a dream, the flowers were almost too pretty and the forest was different, almost magical.

"Please, Spinner," Miles implored. "Listen to me! You must wake up. I know that sleeping feels better, but the pain won't go away just because you sleep. You must wake up or you will be killed by the trolls."

Maybe that wasn't such a bad idea, I'd just sleep and never wake up again. No more pain or sadness, I thought dreamily. I felt like I was floating on a cloud, it was so soft.

"*Spinner*," Miles screamed, "you don't want to die. You will live a long happy life, I promise. But you have to try. Nothing in life is easy, Spinner. Everything takes work. Now wake up, or do you want Tump to die too? Open your eyes!"

In a few seconds Miles started to fade away. The last thing that I saw were his translucent eyes. The funny thing was, I couldn't remember what he looked like—just my luck.

When I woke up, my leg was throbbing. I couldn't get up without Tump's help.

"Tump," I yelled. "Come here, we have to get moving. The trolls are gaining on us, so please help me up."

Tump picked me up with ease. I leaned on him while he positioned my crutch under me. I took a step and almost screamed. I had never felt pain like this before. It was almost more than I could bear, but I would walk as long as I was able. Every step was agony, my leg was bleeding again and the poison was still doing damage. My breathing was labored, and my heart was beating way too fast. I knew that I had a fever and I was so thirsty.

Chapter Eleven

As we walked, I noticed that the landscape was changing. The path was firm, no more soggy ground. I smelled fresh air. Even Tump was acting happier. He said he was glad I was feeling better, and he knew that it wouldn't be much longer and we would be free of the bog. I wasn't about to burst Tump's bubble, but I wasn't better.

I saw the edge of the bog first. The clearing was beautiful. Open fields stretched as far as the eye could see. The sky was breathtaking. I almost cried. I had thought that I'd never see it again. It was the most beautiful blue I had ever seen. The sight of all this energized me.

I called to Tump, "Let's go, we have a lot of open ground to cover. We are an easy target until we get across this field."

So off we went, weaving through the tall grass. Tump was in awe. It had been so long since he had seen the sky.

"Oh, Spinner, if we were to die right now, I'd go with a smile on my face. Look at the clouds. They are so white and puffy. I had almost forgotten what they looked like. Thank you Spinner, for hanging in there with me. You don't know what this means to me!" Tump cried.

I understood what Tump was feeling, to a certain extent. I had only been without the bright sunlight for several days, but my heart had still skipped a beat when I saw it. I couldn't believe that the golden rays could have such an effect on me. I wanted to stay and soak in them all day, but I knew that we had to go. On the other side of those mountains, the dark forest awaited.

"Come on, Tump, you have the rest of your life to look at the sun." I wasn't too sure about me, my fever was even higher, and my whole body was burning from the poison. My stomach had started to cramp and I was getting weaker. I knew we had to get across this field before we were spotted. I didn't know if it was my imagination, but I thought I heard muffled voices approaching.

As we walked, I couldn't help thinking about my dream. Miles, and what he had told me, seemed so real. I didn't know what Miles was, but I knew that he had special powers. He could see into a different world, a world full of magic. I knew that Miles was probably the most powerful being I had ever met. I was jealous and resented him for that. But at the same time I cared greatly for him, and I knew that he felt the same way about me. Being a spider isn't easy, almost every insect in the forest is a meal to me, so it was hard to have friends. It would have been easier if I had some self-control. If I ever made it home, I would try to change.

The meadow was heavy with the aroma of flowers. Lilies dotted the field. I wished we could stop and enjoy it. I was holding onto Tump for support. The splint wasn't really helping my leg, especially when I walked. The broken ends were still grinding against each other, and the pain was horrible. The gouges in my back and shoulders stung and burned. The cramps in my stomach had increased. I still felt the scorpworm's poison moving through every part of my body. I really just wanted to rest, but for now, that was out of the question.

Everything started to get black, and down I went. When I came to Tump was shaking me, calling. "*Spinner*, please don't die on me!" Tump yelled as he shook me.

"Tump, don't shake me," I said in a weak voice. "I just can't walk any farther. You are going to have to go on without me. Once you get across the Black Mountains, you should be able to find your way home easily."

I was gasping for air. I hoped Tump could understand me. The blackness engulfed me again and I was asleep.

In my dream I was sliding down a slippery hill. We used to play on a hill like that near the pond by my tree. Down we would slide, splashing into the muddy water. Little by little I floated up from my dream. Where was I? My vision started to focus. I was being dragged along the ground. Tump had come to the rescue again. He had laid me on a big green leaf and was pulling me behind him. When I thought of the trouble he had gone to, my heart swelled with thanks.

"Tump, I told you to leave me. I'm slowing you down too much," I said.

"I can't leave you behind, Spinner. We are a team, and besides a friend doesn't leave a friend especially when he needs help. I'm here for you in good times as well as bad," Tump said with a goofy smile on his face. "I'm glad that you are awake. I was getting tired of talking to myself. How do you feel, are you any better?" Tump asked.

"I just need some rest, Tump, then I'll be fine. How long have I been asleep, Tump?" I hated to lie to Tump, but why worry him right now?

"Oh, I'd say about two hours. Look! You can see the mountains real good now," Tump answered.

I turned my head, which took a lot of effort. My neck was stiff and my head was throbbing. My eyesight was blurry, but I could see the mountains looming before us. They *were* black, and the jagged peaks seemed to touch heaven. The tops of the mountains were so high. You could see clouds circling them. The snow was so white that it hurt your eyes as it blanketed the top of the mountain.

I would never make it over the mountains. My strength was just about gone. I doubted that I could even stand on my own. I had to make it to the edge of the mountain for Tump's sake. I had to show him the way over it.

"Okay, Tump, can you pull me a little farther."

We were almost through the meadow. Tump started pulling me once again. He was humming to himself as he walked. I wished I could be more like him. He acted like he didn't have a care in the world. You never would have known he had almost been killed that morning. We came to the edge of the meadow about an hour later. I told Tump to stop and rest while I surveyed the area. I had to figure out the best way for Tump to get over the mountain. There had to be a pathway across it. Tump started to hunt for food. He must be hungry, pulling me would be hard on an elephant.

I waited until Tump was out of sight, then I slowly got up. I let out a moan as I straightened up. My vision blurred again for a few seconds, so I took a few deep breaths. As my vision cleared, I started to limp around to get a better look at the mountain. Huge boulders had fallen down to the ground and broken up into hundreds of pieces. I had never seen rocks so black before. There were trees scattered here and there around us. Then I saw a very narrow path that seemed to weave its way up the side of the mountain. Cliffs jutted out along the path. I wondered how long it had been since that path was used. It looked like there were caves here and there along the path. They would be good shelter at night. Maybe Tump could make it out of here on his own! When he returned I would break the news to him that he would be making the rest of the journey alone. I wasn't being brave, just practical. He sure couldn't take care of me, much less carry me across the path, too. It would break my heart to make Tump go on, but it was the right thing to do.

Tump showed up with two fat ticks. He had also filled the acorn top full of water for me. He had a proud look on his face as he handed me one of the ticks.

I looked at it and gagged. "Listen Tump, I can't eat this right now. You go eat yours, I'll eat mine later." I greedily drank the cold water. My stomach went into spasms, but I didn't care, it tasted so good and cooled my hot throat. Tump walked over to me and put his arm around me.

"Spinner, you have to eat something. You can't live on water alone," Tump said.

"You go eat and then we will talk, okay Tump?" I said.

Tump agreed and sat down to eat his meal.

Tump finished and came back over. This was going to be the hardest thing I had ever done. "Tump, I want you to sit down and listen to me. And please don't say a word until I finish." Tump looked up at me with his big sad eyes and nodded. "I found the way you need to go to get across the mountain." I pointed to the path. "That is the way. It should lead you across and down the other side of the mountain. Now I know that you are not going to like this, but you must do as I say." I took a deep breath and continued. "I'm hurt bad, Tump. I won't be able to go with you. I can only walk a few steps at a time. There isn't any way I can make it across the mountain with you," I sighed.

"*Noooo,*" Tump screamed, "if you can't go, neither will I. I won't leave you here Spinner," Tump cried, "I just can't."

"When I fought the scorpworm I was poisoned. That is why I can't eat, see, or breathe very well. There is just no way I can go any farther. Tump, you are going to have to be brave and do the right thing. I didn't save you from the scorpworm so that you could die with me. Please don't let all I did be for nothing. I'm begging you, Tump, go on. Find your way home, for me." I choked up and couldn't say any more.

I braced myself for Tump's reaction. Tump got up and lunged for me and I recoiled. I sure didn't need any more injuries.

Tump grabbed me firmly, but gently by my shoulders and said, "You are going with me! You don't have any choice, because I'm not staying here, and I'm not leaving you behind. So don't argue with me, save your strength."

Tump pulled the leaf over by me and lifted me onto it. He put the acorn, full of water, down beside me and off we went. I was extremely angry and relieved all at the same time. I didn't argue with Tump, I was too weak and tired. I knew that my loyal friend would die for me, as I almost had for him.

Chapter Twelve

Black Mountain loomed ahead. I prayed that we wouldn't run into any trouble; I couldn't handle much more. Tump slowly pulled me along the path. Higher and higher we climbed. I could see the whole meadow below. The wind was blowing through the green grass, making it ripple like waves. My eyes suddenly snapped back to the left end of the field. The hair on the back of my neck stood up and a chill ran through me. The trolls were coming. And from the speed at which they were traveling, it wouldn't be long before they'd be at the foot of the mountains. I yelled for Tump to stop, and pointed in their direction.

"What are we going to do Spinner?" Tump asked worriedly.

"Let me think for a minute, Tump," I answered.

I knew that we couldn't outrun them. The path was starting to narrow quite a bit. If the trolls started up the path, we were finished. We had just passed through an area like a canyon. I could see loose rocks piled up on both sides. If I could get up there and start an avalanche, I could block the only way up to where we were. It was a shaky plan, but it was the only one I could come up with. Tump was not a climber, so I would have to be the one to do it.

"I'll protect you Spinner, don't you worry," Tump said proudly.

"No, I know what to do, Tump," I said.

I got up using my crutch and made it over to the bottom of the rock wall.

"Tump, you stay back." I had already explained my plan to him.

If it went right, the rocks would fall away from us, but there was always a chance that they could fall the wrong way. I grabbed the rock ledge and pulled myself up. I was covered in sweat and breathing too hard from this small effort. I wished I could kill that scorpworm again for what he had done to me. I grabbed another rock and went farther up. Inching myself along, I found a somewhat sturdy place to stand among the loose rocks. I tested the rocks to my right. They moved fairly easily. I had told Tump I was going to block the path, but that wasn't going to be enough. I knew that we needed to stop the trolls in their tracks or they would never quit pursuing us.

Waiting is hard for a spider. We have to wait for food to come to us. I had a reputation at home. Since I was so impatient, many times I would go ahead and tackle my prey. I'd swing from my web and catch flies in mid flight. I would jump on top of ants or roaches. My parents said I embarrassed them. No respectable spider would resort to such methods of using these means to capture his meal. I never went hungry, though. Well, if they could only see me now. I hadn't eaten in days, and I wasn't the least bit hungry. Wouldn't my parents be proud of me! So I now sat and waited for a different kind of prey. I wouldn't eat those rotten little trolls, but I'd do my best to hurt them, or worse. I wouldn't let them scare Tump again.

I didn't have to wait long, they appeared in the clearing near the path. It looked like our friend, Gulp, had been busy and had a little bit of fun with them. I didn't know how many they started out with, but only five remained. And what a mess they were. Stinky, the one that I had run off at the bridge, was missing two or three fingers. He was covered in green slime and looked miserable. Three of the others were so muddy, it was hard to tell if they were walking backwards or forwards. The leader had a mean-looking face that just oozed authority. He had a rotten confidence about him that I didn't like at all. He was the dangerous one. If I could take him out I knew that the rest would run. As they came closer I could hear the leader shouting orders to the others. He would turn around, lunge for one of them, and they would all cower away. Stinky was holding what was left of his hand protectively to his chest. I'll bet he was wishing now that he'd kept his mouth shut.

"Hey, Spinner," Tump yelled, "why are you taking so long.... What are you doing?"

"Shut up, Tump! I hissed, do you want to get us killed? Just stay back."

The leader turned my way and yelled, "Are ye still alive up there? Not for long, I be coming for ye and will eat ye for dinner."

I laughed at him. "Well look at what I get to play with. A smelly little toad and his friends. Did you see your friend, scorpworm, on your way here? I played with it, too. But, alas, it gave out," I said in what I hoped was a strong voice.

The leader's eyes grew bigger. *Good*, I thought, he had seen the dead scorpworm.

"Ye didn't kill the scorpworm, a dragon took the life from it. Ye has lies coming from ye's mouth," the leader spat.

"Oh, I killed your scorpworm friend by yanking out its heart. Just like I'm going to do to you. So come on, I'm hungry."

At first the leader of the trolls seemed to hesitate. Then, in a fury, he charged up the path. The others followed behind him, but they moved more slowly. Great, he was mad; I knew he would be careless, and that was to my advantage. I laughed at the troll, which angered him more. He was now screaming horrible words that I had never heard before. This made me laugh even harder. *Come on*, I thought, *just a little closer*. The troll was running at breakneck speed up the path. As I applied pressure to the rock, gravel under it sifted to the ground. I pushed harder and the rock started to move. Just then my vision blurred and everything around me started to go dark. Not now, I screamed to myself. I grabbed my broken leg and squeezed, the sharp pain snapped me back to reality. I gave the rock one last push and down it went. The rock fell into other rocks and started an avalanche. The troll saw the avalanche too late. The rocks slammed into the leader and knocked him to the ground. He didn't move or utter a sound. The other trolls took one look at him, turned around, and ran. I sat back, leaning against the ledge, feeling the coolness of the rock. I wish it hadn't come down to this, but I knew if the trolls had gotten to us, we would have been their dinner, just like the leader said.

I hated this senseless killing. Yes, I kill for food—there isn't a choice. I hated this savage place with all of its horrible creatures. I let out a long sigh and climbed down. Tump was patiently waiting for me.

"Did you stop them?" Tump asked.

"Yes," I said in a heavy voice, "they won't bother us anymore."

The world around me went black again. This time I didn't fight it. I welcomed the darkness.

THE CAVE

Chapter Thirteen

Time is a funny thing. I know it takes sixty seconds to make a minute, and sixty minutes to make an hour. But sometimes a few seconds seem to last for hours, and sometimes hours seem to last mere seconds. When I opened my eyes, we were in a cave. It was dark and cool. Tump was sitting next to me and resting. The walls of the cave had a strange kind of moss on them. The moss was glowing in a light pink color. The mouth of the cave was a small pinpoint of light. I could still see fairly well. Huge stalagtites dripped down from the ceiling in all sizes. Outside I could hear rain, and thunder boomed throughout the cave.

Tump looked over at me with an anguished face and asked, "Oh, you are finally awake. Do you want water or something to eat?"

"No, not now," I answered.

"I know that you need medicine, Spinner, but I don't know how to make it for you. I can't help you, and I know that if you don't get help, you might die. If I wasn't so stupid maybe I could help you. Please tell me what to do," Tump pleaded with me.

I nodded at him and said, "Just get me some water, please, and then I'll figure out what to do next."

Tump went to get me some water. I looked up at the ceiling and called out to Miles. "If you really can help me, Miles, now is the time. Because I'm out of ideas and strength."

Tump came back with a cup of cool, clean rainwater. He helped me sit up and I drank it in one gulp. It tasted so good!

I put the water down and looked at Tump. "You are a good friend, and I know that you would do anything to help me. But I don't know what to do, either. We will just wait and rest." I lay back down and drifted off to sleep.

Much later I heard a conversation, which woke me up. I opened my eyes and saw Tump talking. But I was too weak to sit up, so I couldn't see very clearly. I turned my head and saw Miles floating in front of Tump. Now a shimmering gold glow was radiating off of him, and his big eyes were silver, just as in my dream. His voice was strong and kind at the same time. He was saying in a fatherly voice, "Now Tump, go into the cave deeper and find those plants I described to you."

Tump jumped up and said, "Okay Miles, I'll be back as quick as I can. And thank you for helping my friend."

"Spinner is my friend, too. Tump, I'll always be there for him," Miles said.

Tump took off deep into the cave.

"Well, Spinner, nice to see that you are back in the land of the living," Miles said.

"So that wasn't a dream before, it was you talking to me. I don't understand Miles. How can you be here?"

He answered, "Who said I was here? I'm at home in my tree. What you see before you are just shadows and light. With a little bit of magic thrown in."

Now I was getting mad. He just would not give me a straight answer about anything. And right now I thought I deserved one.

"Come on Miles, how are you here? Tell me the truth," I pleaded.

"Okay Spinner, you are right, you do deserve an answer. You have done so much good over the last several days. You are thinking of someone other than yourself, and showing compassion. You put your life on the line to save someone else's. Very admirable, Spinner, you are finally growing up. So here is the answer you want, I am here in spirit only. My body remains behind in our tree at home. I have projected my spirit here, to help you," Miles said.

Now my head was really spinning, how was that possible?

Then Miles said, "All that I can tell you is that I'm not quite from this world. I know that this doesn't help ease your mind much."

I laid my head back down and thought about what he'd just said to me. I sure did have some weird friends.

"Now listen to me, Spinner, you are close to death, but the potion that I'm going to help Tump make will heal you. It will be the foulest stuff you have ever smelled or tasted. You must remember to take a dose two times a day. And don't eat anything until you have taken it all. The potion will make you sleep most of the time, when you do wake up you will be very thirsty. So drink all the water you can. Now go back to sleep, my friend, you need the rest."

As I drifted off to sleep, I heard Miles talking to Tump. Good, he had gotten back okay. I had worried that he might get lost in the cave. Miles was telling Tump how to mix up the ingredients, a little of this and a little of that. Someone was shaking me awake. I wish that they'd let me sleep.

"Wake up, Spinner," Tump said.

I opened my eyes and saw Tump kneeling over me. He had a piece of leaf that had something rolled up inside it. Miles was nowhere in sight so I asked Tump where he had gone. All that Tump would tell me was that Miles had to leave. Tump lifted me up and handed me the potion filled leaf. I gagged at the awful smell, then took a deep breath and swallowed it without chewing. Tump handed me the water and I gulped it down, trying to get rid of that horrible taste in my mouth. I thanked Tump and lay down again.

"Spinner, I'm so glad that you are going to get better. Miles said that it would take some time, but that you would get well. Miles told me exactly where to go in the cave to find the plants he needed to make the potion. And do you know what? I didn't even get lost, and I wasn't scared. How did he know where to tell me to look? He told me that he had never been in this cave before. So how did he know, Spinner?" Tump asked.

"I think that Miles has forgotten more than we will ever learn, Tump. I have known him for years, and he is never wrong. Have you eaten anything, Tump?" The potion was starting to make me sleepy, and I was tired of talking.

"Not yet," Tump said, "but I know where some cave bugs are."

I told him to go get them and eat while I rested. Tump patted me on the shoulder then got up. Everything was out of focus now, and I was drifting off to sleep. For the first time in days I didn't hurt at all. *Miles sure is a great doctor*, I thought as I went to sleep.

Tump woke me up twice a day to give me my medicine. At the time it seemed like he was waking me up every hour. Like I said earlier, hours seemed like minutes. I think that I drank a whole lake of water. It tasted so good. On what I found out later was my eighth day, I woke up on my own, feeling so much better. Tump had to help me up; I was still shaky, but it felt good to move around again. Tump showed me around the different rooms of the cave. He led me to a crystal clear stream that ran through the caverns.

"This is where I have been getting your water. Miles told me it had something called minerals in it that would be good for you. He said that it would make your leg heal quicker," Tump said with that silly smile of his.

I bent down and drank deeply. I would miss this water when we left. The cave walls were so smooth and shiny in here. As we started back, I felt my first pang of hunger. I was through with my medicine, so we ate some cave crickets. We headed back and I took a nap. We decided to leave the next day, early the next morning. I hoped the worst was behind us.

Chapter Fourteen

The sun was coming up when we left our cave. I was using my crutch, so off we went. I was pretty proud of myself. I walked at an easy pace without any assistance. Tump was beaming. I had thanked him earlier for all his help and told him that I knew I would not have survived without him. The path on the mountain headed steadily up. We walked until midday then stopped to have lunch. Tump had brought some cave crickets with him. He also had a surprise for me. Somehow he had managed to make a pouch out of a leaf. He had filled it with water from the cave. He smiled as he handed it to me.

I couldn't believe this and said, "Thank you, Tump, you are so thoughtful."

When we started out again, the path had become bumpy and very narrow. I was more at ease on this kind of terrain than Tump. Even with my bad leg I moved easier on the path than he could.

I was leading the way and stopped. "Here, Tump, take this web and tie it to yourself. It should make you feel more at ease walking this high up."

Actually, I did it in case he fell over the side. If Tump fell, I hoped I'd be able to pull him up. The path narrowed even more. If it got much worse, I was afraid we would have to turn back. I told Tump to look straight ahead, and not over the side. It was at least two hundred feet straight down. The temperature had dropped at least twenty degrees since this morning and the air was thinner. I had to breathe deeper and deeper. The air must have a lot less oxygen in it up there. I turned around to check on Tump. His eyes were glassy. I made him sit down and take long deep breaths. His head finally cleared and we got up. Tump was clearly too scared to go much further.

"There must be a cave around here somewhere; we'll walk until we find some kind of shelter and then quit for the day," I said.

It had been a long day and my leg was hurting, so I had decided that we would knock off early.

A half-hour later I found a cave. It was about ten feet above the path, which meant Tump would have to climb.

"I can't climb up there, Spinner, I'll fall over the side," Tump said.

"No, you won't, I'll help you up," I offered.

I climbed to the entrance of the cave and sat down. I grabbed the web that was tied around Tump and pulled him up. Tump was relieved to be safe. This cave was a lot smaller than the last one. I noticed orange flowers growing out of the cave walls. I walked over and touched one. It was hot to the touch. I picked a bunch of the flowers and laid them in a pile in the back part of the cave. We sat around it and warmed ourselves. Tump found some more cave crickets and we ate in silence.

"I think that we are close to the top of the mountain Tump," I said to break the silence. But Tump didn't respond. "What is wrong Tump? Why won't you talk?"

Tump looked up at me with a sick look on his face. "I'm dizzy, no matter what I do, it won't go away."

"It's the altitude, Tump; you have to breathe slow and easy. Once we start going down the other side, it will go away."

We were in a small chamber inside the cave, far away from the entrance. Even two hours after the flowers were picked, they still glowed and put out heat. That night we were warm and toasty.

We got up early the next morning. We ate our breakfast and headed to the entrance. It was gone! A white wall had us blocked in. *Oh no, it must have snowed last night,* I thought. Tump looked worried and very uneasy. I walked over to the entrance and started digging. It didn't take long to work my way through. I looked down and saw that the path was still visible. But now that it was snow-covered, it would be so much harder to travel on.

I walked over to the cave wall and picked a big pile of the orange flowers that Tump had already named "glow petals," and stuffed them into the empty water pouch. The cold wind was blowing through the hole I had dug out. I could tell that Tump wasn't looking forward to the cold walk ahead.

"Well, Tump, it's time we got moving, we need to get home," I told him.

"I don't know, Spinner, it's awfully cold out there. Why don't we stay here until it quits snowing?" Tump said hopefully.

"No, Tump, we can't stay around here any longer. The snow might not let up for days, and if we wait much longer we may not be able to find the path again. Besides, once we start down the other side, it should warm up."

At least I hoped it would. I had no idea what would be on the other side of this mountain, but it had to be better than this.

We walked over to the mouth of the cave, and I slowly lowered Tump down to the path with a strand of my web. He landed in the soft white snow and almost disappeared. The snow was a lot deeper than I thought. I joined him and we started walking.

"Tump, you are the only spider that I have ever known who was afraid of heights," I told him.

"I can't help it, I'm a ground spider," Tump said, blushing.

We made very slow progress; the snow was deep and the wind was getting stronger. I tethered Tump to me with a piece of web, just in case he fell. It started to sleet about two hours into our walk, which slowed us down even more. I had thought we would have been to the top of the mountain by now, but we were still heading uphill. Walking was getting impossible, the snow was up to my waist, and a hard layer of ice had formed on top of the snow. So we had to break through the hard crusty top layer as we moved. My hair was frozen and my eyes burned and watered. I was now pulling Tump behind me. He was shivering so badly that he couldn't even talk. I had to find a place where we could rest for a little while and warm up.

My stomach was growling terribly. I would have given anything for a slug or tick. I had been hunting for a place to rest but couldn't find anything. The wind was getting stronger and every breath that I took froze my lungs. The sleet had turned back into a heavy snow, which was making it impossible to see. Around the next sharp turn, the path widened quite a bit, which made it a lot easier to maneuver. I was worried about Tump, no matter what I said he only answered in grunts. I knew that I had to get him out of the cold. All I could see was white. I felt like I was going blind. There was a small outcropping of rock up ahead, so I told Tump to stop while I checked it out. I had come up with a plan, not a great one, but it would have to do. I piled snow under the outcropping until I filled it up. I tunneled into the pile and made a cave. It wasn't great, but we would be out of the icy wind and snow. Tump was standing where I left him, I hollered for him to come over and crawl inside. I got out the glow petals and laid them in the middle of our cave. Tump finally started to come around, he moved closer to the flowers and sighed. It was actually getting warm in there; the snow and ice were melting off our hair, and I could finally feel my legs.

"Boy, Spinner, I wouldn't have lasted much longer out there. I didn't know it could get so cold, I'm so glad that we stopped," Tump remarked.

"You should have told me how bad you felt, Tump, I would have stopped sooner," I told him.

"I didn't want you to think I was a sissy," Tump said with a sad face.

"Tump, this journey is dangerous, I almost died after that fight. So you have to promise that you'll be honest with me, I'm your friend. I'd never think less of you; if you were tired or feeling bad, you should have told me. In this cold you can get frostbite and lose a leg. You can die out there in this weather, okay?"

"I promise, Spinner, I'll tell you from now on if I feel bad or get tired."

A little while later Tump had fallen asleep, and I was glad. I needed time to think. This whole adventure had been a mess. I had no idea if we were going the right way. Maybe this mountain just keeps going up and up to the heavens. The spark of anger I had in me was growing. Why me? What did I ever do to deserve this? I wanted to be home now, on my tree in the bright sunshine. I was so tempted to go to the edge of the cliff, let out a long string of web and balloon home. I knew that I could soar above the low clouds and be home in no time. I looked at Tump and resented him, which made me feel bad. I knew that Tump would never leave my side. He had stayed and taken care of me while I was sick. But then the nasty side of me thought, *What else could Tump do? He is lost without you, he'd never find his way home, or back to where we had started.* Oh, I was so miserable. I hated myself for these thoughts, but I also knew what I was thinking was true. I always knew I was a rotten spider, but the thoughts I had were downright hateful!

I heard the wind and snow blowing outside and shivered just thinking about it. I had filled in the opening of our cave with more snow, so the snow wouldn't blow in. The flowers were glowing a bright orange and putting out an incredible amount of heat. I guess the more flowers you piled together, the more heat you got. The inside wall, which was getting most of the warmth, had melted enough to be smooth as glass. The only thing missing was food. My stomach was growling like a bear. I had lost a lot of weight during my illness, and now wasn't a good time to go without food. But I knew there was nothing around here to eat, so why bother going out and hunting. We had to get off this mountain before we starved or froze to death. For Tump's sake, I knew that I had to be strong, and at least act sure of myself.

But as I sat alone staring at the flowers, I thought again about leaving. I knew if we didn't get relief soon, I would. The temptation was getting harder to resist. Let's face it, I've always been self-centered and spoiled. Yes, I had Harley and Miles as friends, but really, when it came down to it, I kept them around just for my amusement. They were someone to talk to when I was bored. I didn't really like or dislike them. I loved my family, but how often did I see them? Once or twice a year, at the most? It was easier not to care. Then I didn't miss them. All that really interested me was my next meal. Now that was pure enjoyment, waiting and watching. Then jumping out like lightning and catching my prey. My life at home was complete, or at least it had been. Now I wondered if I would get the same enjoyment from the simple things. Or even worse, would Tump want to stay near me forever. I had always been a solitary creature. How would it be with a constant companion? Too much to think about, and I was getting tired. I decided to push that all aside. I'd figure it out some other time. It was time to sleep. I needed the strength.

Chapter Fifteen

I was almost asleep when I noticed a glowing light. At first I thought it was the flowers, but no, they glowed orange. This light was a bright, white blue! *What now?* I thought maybe I was dreaming, so I closed my eyes, but I still saw it through my eyelids. *Drat!* Can't even sleep be simple? I sat up and waited for whatever was coming. I should have known—it was Miles. Who else could bother me over long distances!

"Well, Spinner, you are having some nasty thoughts, aren't you?" he asked.

"How do you know?" I growled. "My thoughts are none of your business! Besides I haven't acted on them, have I?"

"No, but you are leaning toward the temptation," Miles said calmly.

What was it with him? He was always so calm, nothing ever got him upset, and believe me, I had tried for years to get him mad. Miles sighed sadly, like a parent would do to a child, which sent me into fits of fury.

"WHY ARE YOU HERE? I don't need you if you won't take us home! I can't even see what you look like. Why is that? Are you afraid to show me the real you? TELL ME, I DEMAND TO KNOW!" I screamed. But even as I said the last word, I could feel my anger ebbing away. When I was around him, for some reason I couldn't make my anger last.

Miles waited for me to get through throwing my fit, as patient as ever. When I was through he started to talk. I noticed that when he talked, the light got dimmer. It must be taking an incredible amount of energy for him to project over this long distance.

I've never talked much about Miles to anyone, and there was a good reason for that: I knew next to nothing about him. He probably knew everything about me; no, I take that back, he *did* know everything about me. I was positive that he could read my mind, so I could hide nothing from him. That was another reason for my anger toward him. Why and how did he know about every aspect of my life, and yet I wasn't even allowed to see his face? Would I turn to stone? Was it so hideous that I'd lose my mind or run screaming for my life? Or was he so beautiful and full of wisdom that I'd never leave his side? I had no way of knowing since I had no choice in the matter. I wasn't used to being treated like that. I have a very forceful personality and can usually impose my will on anyone. But not Miles, and that angered me beyond reason! But I also knew in my heart that I would learn about him somehow, no matter what it took.

Miles patiently waited as I sorted all this through my mind. I could tell he was amused by my thoughts, the rat!

"Well Spinner, are you ready to talk to me?" Miles said in his musical voice.

"What do you want, why are you bothering me? I need all the rest that I can get," I growled.

"I'm here," Miles said, "because you are thinking seriously about leaving Tump behind. And that can't happen, he is too important."

"What do you mean? He is just a silly spider. Yes, he matters, but you act like without him we all would perish." I was trying to figure out what Miles meant about Tump.

"Spinner, I am not allowed to explain such things to you. But this you must believe—Tump is very important. There are higher powers at work here, and he must be brought home safely. So that he can fulfill his purpose, and the cycle can continue. Do you actually think that you ended up in that forest by accident? That you just stumbled upon him?"

I couldn't believe what Miles was saying. I was too stunned to speak at first. I was trying to process everything Miles had just told me.

"Are you telling me someone or something sent me into this horror on purpose? What am I? A puppet? Pull the strings and watch Spinner perform!"

I had never felt so much anger and hatred in my life. I jumped up so fast not even Miles saw it coming and lunged in the direction of his voice. Of course I just grabbed air, but he let out a small scream, and that pleased me more than words could say. I turned toward the door and smashed through it.

Chapter Sixteen

Outside, the snow and wind felt good on my face. It stung, but at that moment I would rather have been out there than inside, listening to my traitor friend. Why did I call Miles a friend? He probably knew everything that was going to happen. I felt used, and right now I hated them both, Tump and Miles. Even though Tump knew nothing and was innocent, I felt that he was being used by Miles and his friends. I had to somehow sort through it all and make some sense out of this. So off I went, into the blinding snow. I knew that Miles would take care of Tump, and if I didn't come back he would find a replacement. Apparently, this was Miles's mission. Get Tump home at all costs. So I continued into the storm, not caring what happened.

I am no ordinary spider. I am very different from other spiders. I can trace my family back for thousands of years, and we have grown stronger with each generation. I am faster than any insect alive. I am stronger than my father and my older brothers. As far as the rest of the insects, they think I am a normal spider. I have no enemies. There is no other insect that can kill me. They may be able to hurt me severely, but I will survive. I have never worried about being killed in our part of the forest. Our relatives have always been careful not to let a human capture them. We make our webs like other spiders, though when it comes down to it, we really don't need them. I can look at any insect and make it do what I want. My mother had said that spiders like me are very rare. There aren't many of us left, so we keep to ourselves. We are not noticed. Our kind was around when the dinosaurs roamed the earth.

So why did I have such a hard time dealing with Miles? Maybe he was my equal and I didn't like it. Maybe he was even more powerful than me. I kept walking through the snowstorm with no destination in mind. I felt so betrayed. Miles should have asked me to help Tump. I probably would have refused, but at least it would have been up to me to decide. How could Miles call me his friend and not tell me what was going to happen? I can handle almost anything, but a friend lying to me was just too much. My first thought was to leave them. I was sure Miles could find some other sucker to help Tump get home. I don't need friends to be happy, and I sure didn't need this added responsibility. I didn't ask for it; I was tricked into this whole mess. It really wounded my pride to be fooled. And it made me hate Miles even more.

On I walked, enjoying the snow as it stung my face. This was something I could deal with—the cold wind was honest, it didn't deceive me. I wanted to hurt something, tear it apart, but unfortunately nothing was within my reach. I knew I had a big decision to make and I called out to my mother. I was hoping that she could connect with me somehow. She was wise and the one creature in this world that I truly trusted. I waited but got no response, I was probably too far away for her to pick up my thoughts. I felt totally alone.

I decided I had to confront Miles. It was time to have it out, once and for all. The weird thing was that I wasn't even scared. I knew that Miles had immense power, and that he could probably destroy me with a single thought, but I didn't care. He would have to hear me out.

Chapter Seventeen

I hadn't realized that I'd gone so far. I knew that I was walking in the right direction, but my tracks were gone. The wind howled and the snow was coming down so fast and thick that you couldn't tell the ground from the sky. I kept on walking, and an hour later I saw the clearing and our little igloo. I took a deep breath and entered our temporary home. The warmth inside covered me like a blanket. Tump was still sound asleep, and hovering by his side was Miles. The old anger flared in me again, but I pushed it down.

"Well, Spinner," Miles said, "I guess that you are ready to talk."

All that I could see of Miles was a shimmering form that changed constantly. I can't even describe him; the only thing that was constant were his large amber eyes. They were so soothing, but it was a trick. I knew he was trying to calm me down, but I wasn't going to fall for it.

I looked at him and said, "Yes, it is time to talk."

"I am truly sorry that I had to deceive you, Spinner. But the decision wasn't mine alone, there are higher powers at work here," Miles said sadly.

"I'm sorry, that is not good enough," I said with a sneer. "I have a right to know what is going on. I'm the one risking my life, not you or your 'higher powers.' What gave you the right to throw me into this mess without my permission? Didn't you think I had the right to know? What kind of friend are you? Or were you ever really my friend? Maybe it was a setup from the beginning. And what about poor Tump? Does he have any idea that he is here for some important purpose? All he wants to do is go home and be with his family. Will that even happen? Does he even have a choice? Do I have a choice, or is it part of some big plan we have no control over? Give me some answers, I deserve to know," I screamed.

My heart was pounding, and I was breathing hard. If Miles had truly been standing there, I would have ripped him to shreds. But Miles just waited for me to calm down, never saying a word. He sure had a lot of patience.

I was glaring at him, waiting for some response, when he started to speak.

"I know that you are upset with me. But don't ever doubt that I am a true friend. I have always cared for you. But you sell yourself short. Spinner, you are not like other spiders. You care! You think about the larger picture. Most insects go through life with just three purposes. To eat, not be eaten, and to increase their numbers. They cannot think beyond that. If a brother or sister gets killed by another insect or animal, most spiders don't particularly care one way or another. Your family cares about each other. Tump's family does, too. Think about it, your family and Tump's have accomplished something very rare. You understand that there is more to life. You know that there is a huge world with wondrous creatures, who live, suffer, and die. Your actions will eventually have an effect on others you have never met, and probably will never meet. That knowledge itself is extraordinary. You need to realize how special you are."

I looked at this creature and sighed. I knew Miles was right. I always looked at things a little differently than my other insect friends. I had learned early on to act as they do. My mother had taught me not to draw attention to myself. To blend in, or my life could be in danger. I am fast and strong, and could outwit any creature. So I kept to myself and got along with the few creatures I associated with. And the rest, well, I ate them!

I glared at Miles and said, "So this gives you the right to throw me in this situation? Without asking me? You were wrong, Miles, no one has the right to do this to anyone. I don't think that I can help you anymore. I'm through with being a puppet!"

With that I turned away from him and sat down. Tump grunted in his sleep and rolled over. Tump really was a kind soul. I had come to care for him immensely. I would not be treated this way by Miles. Not even for Tump's sake—not unless Miles told me the whole truth, which I knew that he couldn't do, even if he wanted to.

I felt Miles at my back and turned. "You are right, Spinner, if I could tell you I would. All that I can tell you is that you were picked for your courage and strength, also, for your intelligence and cunning. We know that you can bring Tump home safely. That is why you were chosen, Spinner. Can you at least forgive me for being a part of the decision?"

"Yes," I answered, "I forgive you for that. But you got me into this situation, and for that I can't forgive you. I didn't have a choice."

Miles looked at me and said, "Do you think that if I had told you what you would be going through, the peril that you would be put in, that you would have agreed? To take care of Tump, another spider that you didn't know very well? Now answer me honestly, Spinner."

I hated it when Miles used logic on me and answered, "You are right. I probably wouldn't have agreed to rescue Tump. But who would? Yes, I see your point of view. But it still isn't fair to me or to Tump. Why don't you just leave us alone and go away? I can't listen to you anymore."

As I said these last words, Miles was gone. I was glad. We didn't need him. I would get Tump home to his family, and if any of Miles's friends tried to take Tump away, I would kill them. I lay down next to Tump and fell asleep, thinking that I had new enemies now. They were fighting for what they thought was a good cause, which was the most dangerous kind of enemy to have. My father had told me that whenever I needed help, I could use powers that I wasn't even aware of yet. I had not needed them at home for any purpose. But this was a different place, and my enemies had changed. I said a silent prayer for help and guidance before I went to sleep. For now I had to worry about getting us off this mountain and finding food. I would figure out the rest when I had to. I drifted off to sleep, dreaming about my home and family.

Chapter Eighteen

The next day we woke up early and hungry. Since there was nothing to eat, we decided to get an early start. I gathered up the glow petals and dug out of our igloo.

Tump asked me if I was talking to anyone last night. I told him that he must have been dreaming. Tump then insisted that he had heard loud voices, but I finally convinced him that it was a dream.

The day was bright and sunny. The layer of sleet was shining like diamonds. There was no wind to speak of, so we made good progress. Tump talked about his family waiting for him at home. He couldn't wait to see them. I didn't know what kind of plans they had for Tump, but I was determined to keep them away from him. What right did they have to decide what he had to do? I would stop them if it killed me. It hurt me that Miles was against me. I had always considered him a friend. Now I didn't know what his intentions were, but if it involved hurting Tump in any way, I considered him a mortal enemy.

As we walked, I remembered something my grandfather had told me he used to do. It was like meditating, he had said. He told me he could go inside himself and tap into some hidden power. At the time I thought he was crazy, but with everything I had just learned, I figured it couldn't hurt. So as Tump rattled on about this and that, I tried it. I thought about nothing in particular. I just let my mind drift. I heard what sounded like a loud *pop*, and the next thing I knew I was floating above my body. I was still leading the way up the side of the mountain with Tump following behind me, but the real me was slowly floating higher and higher above me. I could see the top of the mountain! It wasn't too far ahead of us, and, boy, was I glad of that. I willed myself down the other side of the mountain. There wasn't as much snow on this side, and I figured we would get down a lot quicker than I had originally thought. I soared straight up, just to see how far I could go. I went straight through the clouds, and it was so beautiful it took my breath away. But I started to get scared; what if I couldn't get back in my body? Or I kept floating straight up and couldn't stop? I willed myself back down by picturing myself walking with Tump. And, *pop*, I was back in my body.

All at once I felt the cold air going into my lungs, and the sun was so bright it hurt my eyes. I had to admit, I was glad to be back. But, in a way, I missed the freedom of flight. Tump was still talking about some silly game that he and his brother used to play when they were young.

About an hour later we reached the top of the mountain. We could touch the clouds. Tump was happily dancing around, running through the clouds.

"Oh Spinner, I never thought in my wildest dreams that I'd be able to touch the clouds. I feel like an angel in heaven!"

I had grown to care for Tump so much, his simple ways warmed my heart. I didn't really care for anyone, outside of my family. So the way I felt about Tump was very new to me, and in some ways I didn't like it. With this feeling came a fierce protectiveness toward Tump. I had a sinking feeling that taking care of him would come down to a big fight, maybe to the death. No one was going to harm this simple soul, or use him in some cosmic battle. I didn't know what they wanted from him, but I wouldn't let him get hurt. He was now my responsibility, and I would make sure he got home safe and sound. I walked to the edge of the path, and as I looked down, the clouds seemed to kiss the side of the mountain.

"Okay, Tump, we have been here long enough. We need to start down the other side and find some food."

"Yeah, let's go, I sure am getting hungry," he answered.

We started down the path. It was covered in ice, so we had to go slowly. I didn't want to start sliding, because if I did, I wouldn't be able to stop. The snow we were walking through got thinner and thinner, which made walking a lot easier. We weren't using as much energy, so we made good time. Three hours later we were on a dry path with no snow.

Looking down the path, I spotted a cave, so we went inside. It was a miracle. There were crickets all over the walls. We ate and ate until we couldn't move.

"Let's take a nap, Tump, I'm tired," I said, as we ate the last cricket for dessert.

"Sounds good to me," Tump said with that silly grin.

Chapter Nineteen

We leaned against the cave wall and fell asleep. In my dream, I was being chased by some unseen force. I was running fast through thick, inky darkness. I couldn't see where I was going, or where I had been. All I knew was I was running for my life, and whatever was behind me was catching up. I was almost completely out of breath, my lungs felt like they were going to explode. But I couldn't stop, it was right behind me. I could feel its hot breath on the back of my neck. The darkness that surrounded me seemed to swallow me up. I couldn't gauge my speed because I couldn't see anything. But it felt like I was slowing down, which made me feel even more terrified. Something hit me square in the back, and I started falling. Down and down I went, into nothingness. I knew that if I ever hit the ground, the pain would be horrid. I let out a scream, and woke up screaming. I was covered in sweat, and thought my heart would explode. Tump was sound asleep. It seemed that nothing could wake Tump up, once he was asleep. How was he able to sleep through my screaming? Sometimes I wondered what planet he came from!

I looked around the cave. The walls were covered in green moss. I watched as tiny rivers of water made trails through it. The crickets worked their way through the moss eating it as they went. This was a nice place to rest. Even the ground we rested on was soft, when I moved it seemed to move with me. The world outside didn't seem to exist. Maybe we should just stay here and live. Miles wants Tump out of this strange land. If we stayed here Tump would be safe. We could go deeper into this cave and stay. Well, it was something to think about anyway.

I stared at the mossy wall again, and was starting to drift back asleep when something caught my eye. The water, or what I thought was water, was bright red. It looked like blood running through a vein. I sat up and really looked at this cave, and what I saw didn't make any sense. What I thought were long thin white rocks now looked like ribs. And the entrance of the cave resembled a mouth. But that was impossible. We had gone in the side of the mountain. None of this added up, we were walking down the path when I spotted the cave opening. It was in solid rock. But now I could see a slight shifting in the walls, almost like they were breathing. I looked at Tump, what was it we were lying on? It was a brownish pink...like a tongue. I knew what I was seeing was impossible, but what around here was really normal? All of a sudden, it hit me like a ton of bricks! We were inside some creature! A huge creature! My heart was hammering as I looked at the entrance. It was getting smaller. I grabbed Tump by the arm, not bothering to wake him up. He let out a scream as I flew toward the closing mouth. All Tump could say as he woke up was, "Spinner, what's..."

His voice stopped as he saw the teeth slicing through the opening. They were very sharp, white teeth, and they were twice our size. Our only way out was getting smaller and smaller. As the light outside disappeared, we both dived through the closing teeth. We landed roughly on the path. I looked back and the cave entrance was gone. All that we could see was the solid rock.

"Come on, Tump, we'll talk later," I said as we started running.

We ran down the path, being careful not to touch the rock wall at our side.

"What *was* that, Spinner?" Tump was asking me.

I couldn't answer him, I just kept on moving. I finally slowed down a little while later, and we both started walking.

"I don't know what it was, Tump, so please don't ask for answers." I know that I sounded mean as I answered him.

We walked in silence, and I remembered my dream. I had decided that it wasn't really a dream. It was a warning. Something deep inside of me knew that we were headed for trouble as we had entered that cave that turned out to be a monster. So why did I even go in there? If I had sensed that it could be a trap, why didn't I think before we went inside? I was now questioning everything. Was any thing as it truly seemed? I just didn't know anymore. This was like a nightmare that you couldn't wake from. Did that really just happen to us, or was it an illusion? If I started questioning everything I saw or touched, we could be in big trouble.

Chapter Twenty

It was starting to warm up as we walked further down the path. A slight breeze was blowing. I could smell pine trees. I hoped we would be at the bottom of the mountain soon. I tried to concentrate like I had earlier, to will myself out of my body, but I was too upset. I was still trying to convince myself that we hadn't almost been swallowed by a monster. This was all so foreign, how could it have possibly happened? I decided not to try and figure it out anymore. I had to accept it and move on. Tump was singing quietly to himself, I smiled and thought, *Tump really is a bright spot in all this misery.* He was always happy, which I found quite weird. How could anyone be singing after our experience?

I had to decide how much, if any, I should tell Tump. I knew that he had a right to know what was going on, but I knew so little myself. What could I really tell him?

I took a deep breath and sighed. "Let's stop for a little while, okay, Tump?"

"Sure, Spinner," he said quietly.

Up ahead the path widened, so we could rest without leaning against the rocks. So we sat down, the sun was shining, warming us somewhat.

"Listen to me carefully, Tump. While you were asleep last night Miles came to see me."

Tump smiled and said, "I like your ghost friend, Miles; he seems so nice."

"No, he isn't nice, Tump, and I have decided he isn't really a friend either," I said carefully.

Tump's face looked twisted, and I thought he would cry. This was just what I needed now.

"You are wrong, Spinner, he helped me when you were sick. You would have died if it weren't for Miles! How can you talk this way about such a good friend?" Tump said with tears rolling down his face.

I knew that I had to stay calm and control my temper. Tump had no idea what was going on.

"Look at me, Tump; you know that I'm your friend. I have not left your side since you found me. I have only your best interests at heart. I promised that I would get you home, and I will. But you have to trust me, can you do that?"

Tump slowly shook his head up and down. "Yes, Spinner, I do trust you, but I don't understand what is going on. I thought Miles was our friend. What happened Spinner? Something must have changed last night. Did Miles try to hurt you or something?"

I sighed again. "I'm going to try to explain this to you, but it will take a while. So please don't say anything until I am done, okay?"

"I have known Miles for years, we share the same tree at home. I know this is going to sound weird, but I've actually never seen him. He lives in a hole in my oak tree. All that we have done is talk. He has never come out of his hole. What I am trying to say is, I don't have any idea what Miles really is. I've never gotten a straight answer out of him about anything. The other night when you were asleep, Miles came to see me. He told me that I was sent to help you, to get you out of here. Don't smile, Tump, it isn't what you think. I don't think that their 'purpose' is to send you home to happily be with your family."

"Wait a minute, Spinner, what do you mean 'their'? I thought you only talked to Miles?" Tump asked.

"According to Miles, he is working with others, who have a certain goal in mind. I don't know how else to word this, Tump. I don't know who any of them are, including Miles, or what they really want from us. All I have is a feeling, a very bad feeling. I am positive that we are here for their reasons, whatever they may be. We are being pushed around like pieces on a chessboard. And Miles won't even explain anything to me. I don't like this, Tump. We are in trouble; we are stranded out here with no help," I replied in a shaky voice.

"How do you know that they are bad, Spinner? Maybe they want to help us." I looked at Tump and wanted to pound him into the ground at that moment.

"I just know. Tump, they don't care about us! Can't you understand that? They took us away from our home and families and threw us into this nightmare place!"

I stood up and started pacing around, my voice was getting louder and louder, but I couldn't help myself. I had to get this into Tump's thick head. I had to get Tump totally on my side. He had to believe me completely and be willing to do as I said. I couldn't fight him or have to explain myself at every turn. Tump kept watching me as I paced, with that dull look he'd get when he was trying to figure something out. I jumped in front of him, grabbed him and shook him. I was right in his face, glaring at him.

"You must understand, Tump, this is life and death I am talking about! I am certain that in the end when we have served their purpose, we will die. Or we will die fulfilling their purpose. They have put us in great danger, without batting an eye! When I talked to Miles last night, I felt terrible fear, worse than anything that I have ever felt before. So it is up to you, Tump, either you are on their side or mine. It can be no other way, so you must choose one or the other, *now*."

I walked away, giving Tump a chance to think. It was up to him now, and I was scared. If Tump chose Miles, I would take him to his destination and leave him, no matter how much it hurt. If he chose me, I would find some way out of this mess. I would stick by Tump's side, no matter what. Part of me hoped he chose Miles. I was getting tired of all this nonsense. So I waited for his answer, even though it was hard to be patient.

I felt Tump's hand on my back, and turned around. "I am with you all the way, Spinner. If you say that *they* are bad, I believe you. Whatever you want me to do, I'll do. No questions, Okay, Spinner?"

I smiled at Tump, "Okay, let's get moving. The sooner we get off this mountain, the better." So off we walked down the mountain trail. What awaited us, I didn't know. But from that moment on, we were in this together. It was Tump and I against an unseen force. But I smiled to myself and thought, wait until they get a look at the real me. They have no idea what they are in for.

Chapter Twenty-one

We made it down the mountain before it became dark. At the bottom we could see nothing but a forest of towering pine trees. It had just rained. The air smelled fresh and clean. As we walked through the forest, I could see it wasn't as vast as the forest on the other side of the mountain. As night descended on us, I could easily see the stars. We walked through the trees, and the light of the moon filtered down through the huge branches. I didn't detect any movement in the woods. There was not a single sound from any night creatures. Except for the trees, this forest seemed almost dead. It was so quiet. That bothered me, why weren't there any insects buzzing around? Tump was unusually quiet, too. "What's wrong, Tump? You aren't saying much," I finally asked him.

"I don't know, something is wrong here. This forest seems kind of fake. Like someone made it up. Do you know what I mean, Spinner?" Tump answered.

I looked up at the pine trees. They seemed real enough, with long thick branches of sharp green pine needles. But as I looked on the ground, I figured out what was missing. There were no pine needles on the ground. There should have been a blanket of brown and green pine needles covering the ground. But there were none, just bare earth. This just didn't add up. It looked like an army had come through the forest and picked up every stick, pine needle, pinecone, and clump of dirt that didn't belong.

"What is going on around here!" I yelled.

I started pacing around looking at everything around me. There were no leaves. There were no acorns lying around anywhere. But the worst was the absolute silence. I couldn't hear anything.

75

Tump was shaking. "This place isn't real. Spinner, we are in the middle of nowhere, and I mean, *nowhere!*"

We hadn't walked very far into the forest, but when I looked around I couldn't find the trail we came in on. This was all wrong, and I had an idea who was behind it. It had to be Miles. We had made the decision to defy them, to fight for what we wanted, now they were going to punish us. They were going to show us a little bit of their power.

"Listen, Tump," I whispered. "I have a feeling that Miles and his friends are trying to scare us, so stay behind me and do what I say. Keep your eyes open and warn me if you see anything."

We started to walk very fast through the forest. I was getting madder by the second, and I wanted to tear Miles into a thousand pieces. Up ahead, where the trees thinned out, stood a huge oak. We walked over and looked at it. We crawled inside. It felt real enough, until you looked at the floor. Although it looked like an old tree, there was no rotten wood or wood chips. There wasn't any fungus or termite holes in the tree. We decided to sit down for a few minutes. I told Tump that I was going to rest. Actually, I was going to do just the opposite. I closed my eyes and concentrated on floating up. Nothing happened at first, then that familiar *pop* came. Up I went, through the tree. I could see the wood fibers. Then I saw the bark. Out of the tree I went, climbing higher and higher. When I was over the forest, I stared down at it. It wasn't that big, and beyond the forest was a vast desert. Nothing but sand as far as I could see.

But I wasn't up here to look around at the scenery. I was hunting for Miles and his friends. I thought that if I were in this form, I might be able to see them better. As I scanned the landscape below me, I noticed that the forest was shimmering. It seemed to lighten somewhat, then sharpen into bright colors again. I couldn't see any birds flying through the treetops. Miles was nowhere to be seen, either. Oh well, it was worth a try. I would have to come up with another idea. I concentrated on my body, back down on the ground, and once again I was there. I didn't float down slowly this time. I was there in an instant. I guess I was getting better at this. I was once again next to Tump, who had fallen asleep.

I woke Tump up and we headed out. I told him we had to get out of the forest quickly. Being constantly on guard can wear you out and make you grumpy. I was both. Every noise I heard made me jump. I knew that Miles was behind this fake forest, and I knew we wouldn't get out of here without a confrontation. I almost wished they would come for us and get it over with. I could now see how out of place this fake forest really was. I could rub my foot on the dirt and find sand easily. I was sure if I pushed on a tree hard enough, it would fall over. I grabbed at the pine needles and they fell off the branch easily. When the needles hit the ground, they disappeared. I laughed to myself. Miles didn't do a very convincing job on this place; both Tump and I had noticed the fakeness right away. But I knew that there was a reason for all of this. Tump and I had agreed to stick together and defy Miles and his friends. That made us their enemies. I knew they were going to teach us a lesson as a result.

We had walked for about two hours, when I saw the desert. It was one hundred yards up ahead, just beyond the trees. We were home free. We quickly moved toward the opening in the forest.

"Come on, Tump, ten more feet and we are home free!"

"I can't believe that we made it, Spinner!" Tump said, laughing at the same time.

I started to slow down, but not on purpose. I felt like I was wading through quicksand. Tump was having the same problem: We were moving, but we were going nowhere. Ten feet looked like a mile, and the trees at the edge of the forest were twisting into horrible shapes. Knotholes became twisted screaming mouths; branches were crooked arms grabbing for us. Tump let out a horrible scream. I turned around, in my mind it was very fast, but I was moving painfully slowly. Tump was being lifted by one of those demonic trees. The tree's arms had Tump around the waist. They were lifting him up through the air. Higher and higher he went at incredible speed. I didn't know if they meant to hurt him, or keep him out of the way, so that they could deal with me.

"Hold on, Tump," I screamed. "I'll get you down."

I peered into the forest, looking for any movement. I knew that I'd have to be quick when the attack on me came. I could barely see Tump. Now he was high up in a pine tree tied to the trunk. He was unharmed, but crying.

An unusual calm came over me, and I knew exactly what to do. I would have to wait and be patient. The forest itself had changed in a matter of seconds. It was dark and cold. Thick fog blanketed the ground. All the trees were deformed and twisted now. I knew that we were on Miles's stage. This was his show for now. I tuned out everything around me and concentrated on a tiny spark inside me. Very soon it was a flame. I felt the power flowing through my veins, calming me more. The strength inside me was growing. All that I had to do was wait, and act unsure and scared.

It was so cold now that I could see my breath. I tested my movements and found I could now move easily through the muck that had slowed me down. I moved only a little. I didn't want Miles to know I was free to move as fast as I wanted to. I saw a shimmer in the forest again; everything seemed to jerk and then return to normal. This illusion must take considerable mind power. I knew that Miles couldn't do all of this alone. It must take a lot of power to keep this nightmarish forest solid and intact. I was still scanning the twisted pines for Miles, when at last I spotted him. For a second it turned my blood cold and froze my heart. Well, I had finally gotten my wish. I was seeing Miles as he really was.

Miles still had those big amber eyes, but his body was constantly changing. His legs changed from crablike to long tentacles. His face looked angelic one minute and demonic the next. Horns sprouted out and disappeared just as fast. His skin changed colors and would become transparent. It was a horror to see—fish scales one second and armor plating like a rhino the next. Fur of all colors would sprout and disappear. It was too much for my mind to take in. *Concentrate on his eyes*, I thought. *Don't even look at the rest of him.* I had learned to block my thoughts from Miles. It was quite easy. I just pictured a wall that couldn't be torn down. Brick by brick I added to the wall, making it stronger and stronger. I looked at the thing named Miles and smiled.

"Well, Miles, you finally decided to show up as you really are. I have been waiting for quite a while. I was beginning to think you were afraid to face me. You and your friends didn't do a very good job on this…well, for lack of a better word, 'forest.' Even Tump knew that it was a fake," I said with a laugh.

Miles's eyes grew darker and smaller. I had hit a nerve. Or maybe he wasn't used to anyone standing up to him.

"You think that you know it all, don't you Spinner?" Miles said in a loud, deep voice.

It seemed that when he talked, even the trees shivered. "I told you not to interfere with our purpose. You and Tump can openly defy us, but you change nothing. The elders say that I must teach you a lesson, so you never interfere again. We will take charge of Tump from this point on, I only wish that it hadn't come to this."

If Miles thought he had scared me, he had made a deadly mistake. All that he had done was make me angry. I was in a rage, but I pushed those thoughts away. This wasn't the right time. The red-hot flame had become a bonfire. My heart had slowed down to a steady *thump..thump..thump*. Beating strong and slow. Who did this creature think he was? He would not take Tump from me. Tump was my friend. And as for the purpose, well as far as I was concerned, it had changed.

I glared at Miles and said in an even voice, "Tump is no longer a concern of yours, so, if you know what is good for you, you will leave here right now. Remember telling me the other night that you knew all about me and my family. You are wrong. You know nothing of our past. Or should I say our *hidden* past. You have no idea who you are really dealing with."

This made Miles laugh loudly. Good! I thought I'd be able to catch him off guard. In the blink of an eye, Miles started to change once again. He doubled in size. Six arms grew out of each of his sides. A coat of green hair sprouted. His two legs thickened and long claws popped out of his feet. Long yellow teeth appeared to slide out over his lips. He uttered a deep growl and took a step toward me. He meant to rip me to pieces, but I wasn't afraid. I was focusing all my energy inside. Miles stopped for a minute, puzzled, I guess he expected me to try to run. I smiled at Miles, which enraged him. Six arms lunged at me. I stepped back and easily avoided him. Miles was even madder now. He swung and kicked at me, but he wasn't used to the body that he had chosen, so he was off balance. He promptly fell over to the ground. I laughed so hard that I had tears streaming down into my eyes. I walked up to him and kicked him hard in the side.

Then I leaned down and looked straight into his eyes. "I do not fear you or your friends. Now leave, and take this fake forest with you."

I slowly turned around and started to walk away from him. I wasn't stupid enough to underestimate Miles. My mind's eye was still watching him. Miles slowly got up and brushed the sand off. He had a nasty grin on his face. Slobber dripped off his yellow teeth. He was getting ready to pounce on me again. Just as he was about to reach me, I sidestepped and he went barreling past me. Miles ran face-first into one of the misshapen pine trees and knocked it over. He turned to me and pounced on me before I could move. I grabbed at his throat and my fingers sank into his spongy skin. He was trying to bite me with his teeth, but I was still too fast for him.

"All that you had to do was listen to me," Miles growled, "but you couldn't do it. Everything always has to be your way. Now I have no choice, I have to destroy you, brat spider!"

It is hard to move when you have six arms holding you down. Miles's fangs were closing in on my neck, but I wasn't afraid. I was as calm as I had ever been in my life. Slobber was dripping on my face, but I didn't pay attention to it. I went deep inside myself, and *pop!* I burst out of my body and into Miles's form. I quickly found what I was hunting for. Miles's essence, his spirit. I got a hold of it and ripped it out of his body. Up we climbed toward the heavens, through the forest trees. Past the clouds, up and up we climbed. Miles was now like me, transparent. Fear was written across his face.

"Let me go!" Miles screamed.

But I held on tight, "No, Miles, it's my turn now." I willed myself to climb higher. The clouds were gone. Nothing but blackness surrounded us now. I didn't dare look down. I focused my energy on my grip. I wouldn't let Miles escape now. Everything was dark, except for small white pinpoints of light. Miles was trying to wiggle out of my grip, but having no luck.

"Okay, Spinner, let's talk for a minute. What are you planning to do, rise into the heavens for ever?" Miles asked.

"Maybe, if it will keep you away from Tump," I said with a smile. "And I'm pretty sure I can rip you to pieces in this form. Want me to try?"

We floated in the darkness, going wherever I willed us. It was like being in a black void, completely soundless. I could have stayed up there forever; I was away from all of my problems. Well, almost all of my problems. I still had to deal with Miles, and that was a problem. If I let him live, he would warn the others. I wouldn't be able to catch him by surprise again. If I killed him, could I live with myself? I knew I could hurt him, no problem.

Miles was pleading with me to stop, so I slowed down just a little bit.

"I'm trying to decide if I should kill you, Miles, just like you were trying to do to me in the forest."

"How do you know I didn't kill you, Spinner? Our bodies are still back there, maybe you are already dead."

"That gives me an even better reason to finish you off now," I laughed. "If I let you live, you have to leave Tump and me alone, and get your nasty friends to do the same, convince them. You are so good at that, Miles. We have our own plan, and I won't have you interfering. Don't fool yourself, Miles, I am capable of a lot more than this."

Miles paused and sighed. "They can't be stopped, no matter what you do to me, or what I say to them—they have purpose. They are unstoppable, and very dangerous. I'm still your friend, Spinner, I wouldn't lie to you," Miles said with a small smile.

"You lie," I screamed. "You've never been my friend! We will no longer be your pawns in this sick game. Warn your friends that there is a lot more to me than meets the eye!"

I grabbed Miles and started spinning him around in the blackness. Faster and faster we went, and at the last second I let go of him. Miles went hurtling off into space at an incredible speed. I quickly willed myself back down to the forest. I traveled back down with sickening speed and popped back into my body. The Miles monster was gone!

As a result, the forest was falling apart all around us. I quickly snapped a web up through the branches of the pine tree Tump was hiding in and climbed up to where he was.

"Spinner," Tump yelled, "why wouldn't you answer me?"

The branches that held him were going, and if we didn't get out of this tree soon, we would be standing on nothing.

"Hold on, Tump." I grabbed the web and Tump, and jumped.

We landed just as the top of the huge pine disappeared.

"Hurry, Tump. I don't think standing in this forest is the safest place to be."

We ran out and looked back. I could hear branches giving away with a muffled crack. Thirty seconds later, the forest was gone. Smooth, white sand had replaced it. The mountain path we had come down on ran right into the sand. Tump gasped as he looked around, one second a forest occupied this area, and then nothing. It was a lot for the mind to take in.

"Well, Tump, it looks like we are going to take a walk through the sand."

Chapter Twenty-two

Walking through the sand isn't easy when you have eight legs. The hot sand touches and burns all of your feet, and either you sink in the sand or you are off balance. Keeping your balance turns into a dance of sorts, a few steps to the right, one backward, two to the left.

The sun had disappeared behind the mountains over three hours ago. I knew that we needed to hurry, especially since I had no idea how hot it would get through the day. So for now, night was the best time to travel. Tump kept asking me why I hadn't answered him when we were back in the forest, but I avoided the subject. How could I explain what had happened between Miles and me? So as we walked, I commented on the scenery. The plant life was sparse but beautiful at the same time. Huge cactuses, over twenty feet tall, sprouted out of the sand. They had bright orange, red, and yellow flowers on them. The small thorn bushes that we passed had tiny purple flowers on them, but no leaves, which was odd. It didn't seem very cold, even though it was night. Since we were walking fast, we stayed comfortable.

The sand was as white as snow, and so fine that it was hard to see the individual grains. There wasn't any wind, so it was very pleasant as we walked. However, there was a slight problem: I had no idea where we were going! But for some reason, the way felt right, so I wasn't terribly concerned, at least for now. We walked up and down one sand dune after another. This desert was really vast. Maybe it went on forever, and we would never get across it. At least out here there was no place to hide, so I could see if anything dangerous was coming well ahead of time.

The sand didn't cool off, like I thought it would. Tump was definitely happier out here. He was humming and singing away.

"I like the sand, Spinner. I'll bet that I could dig all the way to the other side of the world. It's so soft and warm, not like the cold mountain or damp forest I used to live in. Don't you love it, Spinner?" Tump asked.

"Sure, Tump, it's just great. That is if you don't mind hot feet, or sand in your hair. Let's hunt for a place to rest, it will be morning soon."

Up ahead I saw a clump of gray rocks that towered at least thirty feet. Surely there was a crack or crevice we could crawl into for the day. We had almost made it to the rocks when the sun started to rise. The bright orange ball seemed to rise straight out of the sand. The sky seemed to burst into a rainbow of colors. It went from pink to orange-yellow to yellow, then, finally, brilliant blue.

It seemed the higher the sun rose, the warmer the sun's rays felt on us. All of a sudden, the color of the sand started to change. It went from being snow white to light pink, and the longer we looked at the sand, the pinker it got. It wasn't an illusion. It really was turning darker. Tump was dumbstruck. He looked around, with his mouth hanging open, and seemed amazed.

"Look, Spinner, it's a rainbow on the ground!"

"Well, now I believe that I've seen everything, Tump," I said with a laugh.

We walked over to the rocks and found a big one that had a crack that ran pretty far back into it. Before we went into this crack, I walked around to make sure we were alone. Then I noticed that the sand was getting cooler, instead of hotter, in the morning sun. We would have to keep watch on the temperature throughout the day. If it didn't get too hot, we'd try walking through the day.

I went inside to check out our newest home. The floor was full of sand, so it would be soft to sleep on. The walls slanted in an upside down V shape. The crack widened toward the back, and it was unoccupied. I thanked the stars. I hoped we could get some uninterrupted sleep. Tump had snuggled down in a small hole he had been digging and was sound asleep.

Chapter Twenty-three

I was too excited to sleep. This desert was very interesting, and I decided to see what else came out with the sun. I went to the entrance and looked out. The sand outside was now bright pink. Inside it was still snow white. I picked up some of the white sand off the floor of our new home and threw it outside the entrance. It landed in the pink sand and immediately started to turn light pink. It took a minute and it was as dark as the rest of the sand. It simply was amazing!

There were three huge cactuses on my right that had bright yellow flowers on them. Then the funniest looking lizard I had ever seen caught my eye. It was bright purple and had orange spikes sticking out of it everywhere. Around each spike there were bright yellow sprigs of hair. It was darting around through the cactus trees. It would go to one cactus and sniff around, then run to the next one. A big wasp zoomed by and the lizard jumped into the air, caught the wasp, and swallowed it before it hit the ground. Its tongue was bright yellow, too. I started to laugh. I couldn't help myself. It turned and spotted me. Oh great, I thought to myself. What if it eats spiders, too. Oh well, too late now. I backed into the cave, but the lizard was at our entrance in a flash.

"Hey man, what's your name? Come on out, dude. I don't eat spiders, too many calories."

I stepped slowly out of the cave. His bright blue eyes were staring at me.

"My name is Spinner, what's yours?" I asked, carefully watching his movements. I didn't know if I could move as fast as he could.

"My name is Dex. When did you get here? I know that I haven't seen you in these parts before."

Dex spoke so fast. It took a minute to digest what he had said.

"We arrived here just a little while ago," I said to this friendly creature.

"We? Who else is in there?" Dex asked, as he moved closer to the opening of our cave.

I answered, "It's my friend, Tump. I'm trying to get him back to our home."

Dex looked inside and saw Tump. Dex was too big to actually walk in through the opening.

"I take it you live around here?" I asked.

"Well, not really, I'm about a two days run from home. I decided to go exploring last week, and well, here I am." Dex said all of this before I could blink my eye. His speech was something to listen to. Up close I noticed that he also had yellow eyelashes. He really was every color of the rainbow.

Dex looked at me with a surprised look on his face and said, "You mean to tell me that you just got here? So you guys walked through the night? Boy, that can be dangerous; don't you know what lurks around these parts at night?"

"No," I said, "we had no idea we were in danger last night. We figured that it was safer than walking during the day."

"No dude! At night the Dark Ones come out. They are bad news. You have no idea how lucky you are. Not too many living things make it through this place at night," Dex said with genuine concern. "If I were you I'd wake up your friend and get moving, or stay until tomorrow morning."

I thought for a few minutes. I didn't like the idea of hanging around here for another day. I had the feeling that time was our enemy. I knew that the Purpose, which is what I was now calling Miles and his friends, wouldn't wait forever to try and destroy me. They knew that getting rid of me was the only way to get control of Tump. Dex could tell that I was having trouble deciding what to do.

His eyes lit up an even brighter blue and said, "I have a great idea. I know that you both are tired, so why don't I give you guys a lift. You and your friend can ride on my back. You can get a few Z's while you ride. I'm ready to head home anyway."

My brain finally caught up with what Dex had just said, "Which way is home for you Dex? Do you heard toward the mountains or the other way?"

"What mountains? I've never seen a mountain, dude," Dex said.

"Oh, that is the way we came from, not a very nice place. I don't recommend going there."

It was a good idea. We could travel and get a little shuteye.

"Are you sure that it wouldn't be any trouble, Dex?" I asked.

"No, like I said, I'm ready to head for home. It will be nice to have some company on the trip back," he replied.

"Thank you, Dex. I really didn't want to stay here another night. But I must warn you. Being around us could be dangerous. We may have some very nasty enemies after us."

"What's going down, man, clue me in?" Dex asked.

I filled him in on my adventure, meeting Tump and trying to get home. I told him about the Purpose, and how they wanted to use Tump, and my fight with Miles.

Dex listened carefully until I was through and said, "Cosmic, man. Sure sounds like you have a lot of weight on your shoulders. It also sounds like you are a good friend to have around."

I thanked Dex, and we went to wake up Tump. He was sound asleep, snoring away. I gently shook him to no avail. So I kicked him, not hard, just enough to get his attention. You must remember that although I'm doing a noble thing by helping Tump, I am still a rotten little spider.

Tump woke up with a start and saw Dex's big blue eyes staring at him. He screamed, of course.

"Calm down, Tump. This is our new friend, Dex. He has offered to give us a ride across the desert. Well, at least to where his home is. He's told me that it is not safe to travel at night. There are a lot of nasty creatures out there," I said firmly.

Tump peeked out of our cave and said hello to Dex. I could tell that they liked each other instantly.

"Hey dude," Dex said, "nice haircut." I guessed that he was referring to Tump's mohawk.

"Thanks!" Tump said with a crooked grin." I know that you guys won't believe this, but I dreamed about you both. You were in trouble, and I helped you out. You looked the same as you are now."

"This must seem like déjà vu, huh?" Dex said.

Or maybe a premonition, I thought. *Nothing would surprise me at this point.* I was ready to believe just about anything. The one thing that I knew for certain was to follow my heart. So far it hadn't steered me wrong.

Getting comfortable on Dex's back was a chore. We had to situate ourselves between his orange spikes, and they were hard and sharp. Tump acted like he rode lizards all the time, he was a real natural. So off we went, Dex moved in a walk-jog. Up and down I bounced, I was really starting to get sick to my stomach. Then it hit me, I hadn't eaten in quite a while. I decided to keep my mouth shut. I'd probably throw up if I ate, anyway. Tump was up front gabbing away to Dex. They were discussing our adventure. Tump was describing the mountains we had just descended. He didn't mention the forest we had come out of last night. I thought this was kind of odd.

I think Tump had figured out that something monumental had happened between Miles and me, but I just couldn't discuss it with him. And I didn't think I would ever be able to explain it to him. It was just too far over his head. Dex had understood what had happened. He had remarked that he had heard of such battles. I hoped that we would have a chance to talk again without Tump overhearing us.

I tried to look at the desert as it passed me by, but it was impossible. The bouncing was making me dizzy. So I held on to the horn on Dex's back and tried to sleep. I really was dead tired. Tump seemed energized from his nap, and gabbed away to Dex. My eyes got heavy, and before long I was dreaming. I was up far above the earth, just floating there, looking around. It was quiet and I was calm. I saw meteors streaking through the heavens. It was awesome. I saw at least fifteen go past, but as each one went by, they were getting closer to me. Soon, they were a little too close for comfort, so I tried to will myself back down to the ground, but I couldn't. I was getting scared. The last meteor had actually seemed to burn me.

Then I heard Miles's soft voice. "You cannot stop me any more than you can stop these balls of fire rushing past you. You are doomed if you stay on this path. Believe me, Spinner, I am your friend and I care about you. But you *must* know that if you fight the Purpose, you will die."

I almost believed him. It was hard not to, we had been friends for years. And deep down inside, I think he really did care about me. But that didn't matter. As Miles had said, I had chosen my path; it was too late to turn back. As the next meteor headed straight toward me, I couldn't move. Closer and closer it came, the heat was burning my fur. With a start, I woke up and fell off Dex's back. It took him a minute to notice that he was shy one passenger. But after a few steps, he stopped.

He looked at me and laughed. "Hey dude, next time you need to stop you can just yell."

I couldn't tell him and Tump that I'd had a nightmare and stupidly fallen off. So I used the excuse that I was hungry.

Tump was hungry, too, so Dex set off to find us some food. Watching Dex catch a meal for us was poetry in motion. Almost immediately he spotted a wasp lingering around a thorn bush. There was a light breeze blowing, it made the pink sand swirl into different shapes, so we lost sight of Dex. He appeared in no time, but I couldn't figure out what he'd done with our food.

"Hey, Dex, what did you do with the food?" I asked.

Dex smiled, popped open his mouth, stuck out his tongue and there were the wasps that he had caught. They were stuck to his tongue. One by one he handed the wasps over to us. Tump gobbled them down at once. I, on the other hand, stared at them with mild disgust. My stomach turned upside down just looking at them, but food was food, I guess. I closed my eyes and ate. Not too bad, considering it came from a lizard's mouth. It hit the spot and I wasn't hungry anymore. I pushed the remains of my dream away. When I tried to figure out the dream, my head spun. I needed a break from thinking. I decided to sit back and study the scenery.

This place was truly a wonder. Nothing was like at home. Even the insects were every color of the rainbow. I loved it. All of the colors and you just never knew what you were going to see next. Dex was busy hunting for more food. I guess it took a lot of food to keep him going, especially since he moved so fast. Tump was pulling petals off of a small violet flower. He turned and smiled at me. It still amazed me that Tump was so peaceful.

Tump looked at me and sighed, "I'm so sorry, Spinner. I know that you never expected all this trouble. If you want to leave me, I won't be mad at you. If you leave you will be safe, and that would make me happy."

"Tump, I went into this with both eyes open, and if I didn't want to be here I wouldn't, you must know that. Besides, I'm not going to be hurt or killed. So don't ask me to leave again, okay?"

I had just closed my eyes when Dex asked me to follow him. "I want to show you something dude; you are not going to believe this."

We walked past a clump of cactuses toward a pile of rocks. There in the center of the rocks was a huge hole. The hole had been dug straight through rock. The smell that drifted up out of the hole was sickening.

"This is where the Dark Ones stay during the day," Dex said in a low voice.

"Is that so sunlight can't hurt or kill them?" I asked.

"Well, no one really knows. I have not heard of anyone stupid enough to go down into one of these holes, much less pull one of the Dark Ones out into the sunlight. Come on man, let's get moving. I want to get as far away from this hole as I can."

We walked back to Tump, and we both climbed on Dex's back again. Dex told us to hold on, and off we went. He was definitely going faster than before. I just wondered how long he could keep up this pace.

Dex told us about his life at home. Apparently it was something like a forest in the middle of the desert. He called it an "oasis." There was a spring right in the middle of it, so they never ran out of fresh water. The trees were tall, but they had no branches on them, just huge leaves at the top of the tree. Dex had never seen a human or a troll. That pleased me. At least I wouldn't have to worry about those creatures. When I asked Dex about the Dark Ones, I could feel him tense up. Apparently this wasn't a subject he liked to talk about.

Dex took a deep breath and began. "The Dark Ones have been around since time began. Now the story that I'm going to tell you has been passed down from father to son for as long as anyone can remember. Before the sun and stars were born there was nothing but darkness. The earth was black and cold. There were odd trees and plants that could live without sunlight. All that lived back then were the trees and plants, a few horrid bugs, and of course the Dark Ones. Back then they could be above the ground since there was no sunlight. But when the sun was born, the entire world changed. At night when the stars came out for the first time, it was to remind the Dark Ones that the sun would never be far behind. The following morning, when the sun rose, the Dark Ones didn't realize that it would hurt them. So a lot of them were killed at first. The rest were driven deep into the ground. The trees that had existed died. The sunlight killed everything that existed above ground. Of course, it was a very long time before any other life appeared. The Dark Ones lived on the lowest forms of life, all the time hating the light and anything that lived above them. For countless years, their hate grew. It even changed their physical appearance. It twisted their bodies and souls. As other creatures evolved, the Dark Ones started venturing out at night. I'm sure it terrified them at first, not knowing whether it would kill them or not. But they learned to go underground before the first light of day. The smart ones survived, but they were still full of hatred. The Dark Ones don't just hunt for food, they love to hurt and kill. They kill whether they are hungry or not. My father told me that his brother had gotten lost and didn't get back to the oasis before dark. When my dad found him the next morning, he was ripped to pieces. Not eaten, just tortured. My father never got over his loss. Now my father and a group of his friends hunt them down at night. They carry torches and burn them. He has seen them. Their eyes are a pale yellow. Their bodies are long and skinny, like their arms. They have long sharp claws and a mouth full of sharp teeth. They are relentless and can't be killed easily."

Dex quit talking and picked up his pace. Deep inside, I knew that Dex was telling the truth. This wasn't a fairy story told by parents to keep their kids from running off. This was all too real. *Great*, I thought, *a new enemy to fight*.

The sun was behind us now, turning a bright orange red. The sand's color was fading from bright pink to a paler version. Soon it would be white again, and hot to the touch. Dex was getting nervous. He had been hunting for shelter for over an hour. Up ahead I spotted a small mound of clay.

"Let's look over there, Dex. Check out that clump," I told him.

The lump of clay turned out to be an old termite mound. It was well over twelve feet tall. It didn't take Tump long to tunnel inside it. The mound was old and crumbled if you hit it.

"Will this do, Dex? It doesn't seem very strong," Tump asked.

Dex walked around the mound and checked it out. "It will have to work. Look! The sun is almost gone."

Tump was already inside looking around when I entered our new shelter. Dex followed, squeezing through the small opening. He was clearly upset, his eyes darting this way and that. There was plenty of room inside, but it smelled really bad.

Dex motioned for us to come closer to him. "Listen carefully and do as I say. Tump, can you close in our door with dirt?"

"Sure, Dex, it'll only take me a few minutes," Tump said as he started to fill in the opening with loose dirt.

Dex was deep in thought as he said, "The smell in here should confuse the Dark Ones. Maybe they won't pick up our scent. And we have to be very quiet. If they find us, we won't be able to keep them out."

Once Tump had filled in the entrance, it was pitch black inside, except for the tiny holes in the side of the mound. I could see that the moon had risen, and outside everything looked quiet. I could see no movement on the white desert sand. But I had a sinking feeling all that would change soon enough.

Dex and Tump sat together in the far corner of our shelter, not talking or moving. I was on guard, watching through the termite holes for any movement. I didn't know what I could do if it came down to a fight, but at least I would know if they were coming. By the size of the hole I saw, I knew they were big. But everything has a weakness, I'd just have to find theirs. I was born to kill. That is what I did best. And I must say that I enjoyed a challenge. So I was pumped for the fight, it would come. I could feel it, a danger not far away. It was out there and I knew that it was coming. We were two forces, bearing down toward each other. Nothing could stop it, and at this moment I wanted the fight. I felt alive, and very strong.

Out of the corner of my eye, I saw something move. The moon was shrouded by the clouds. Only dim light penetrated through them. I concentrated and watched, listening more with my mind than my ears. There it was again, a dark figure moving soundlessly through the sand. I saw an eye flash for a brief second, and then it was gone. I felt, more than saw, it dig into the sand. It planned on coming up right under our feet.

"Tump," I whispered, "dig and open the door, quickly."

Tump didn't hesitate. He dug out a hole in a few seconds.

"Now, Dex, walk outside slowly, and, Tump you get on his back. When I yell '*Dex*,' run as fast as you can. Don't stop or look back, get to your home."

"But, Spinner," Tump stammered, "what about you? How will you find us? We can't leave you here, you'll be killed!"

Dex and Tump were looking at me with pleading eyes. "I'll be fine, now go."

As they started out the door, there was an explosion of sand. Tump screamed as Dex fell forward. He righted himself and almost made it out. But sharp claws caught his side and made a long bloody gash. Dex screamed in pain, I yelled at him to move fast. Dex shot out of the mound and, in a flash, they were gone. The creature was turning under the sand to pursue them, I grabbed hold of its hind leg and bit hard. It yelled and turned its attention to me. Good, now it was my game. I ran out of the mound and went in the opposite direction that Dex and Tump had gone. The creature followed me, but it was having trouble keeping up. I found what I was hunting for, a huge rock. I climbed on top of the rock and waited for the creature to rise out of the sand. It came up with a spray of sand, growling and snarling. "Well, look at this, a fat spider. Ha! What can you possibly do to me?" it hissed.

Dex was right. Its eyes were pale yellow, and they were huge. It had black matted hair, full of dirt and sand. Its claws were long, like they were mostly used for digging. It had a body like a ferret, but with a long, hairless tail. I was totally drawn to its mouth, which was full of long sharp, pinlike teeth. There were too many teeth crammed into one place and it was drooling.

I looked straight into its eyes and said, "I was about to ask you the same question. What are you, a mutant groundhog?"

The creature started to growl and back up. It was going to pounce on me, but just as it leaped into the air, so did I. It landed on one of the rocks, looking around for me. I pounced again and landed on its head and bit its eye. The creature gave out a piercing scream and clawed at its face. I jumped off as it screamed and then rolled onto the sand. I ran as fast as I could, before any of its friends showed up. I headed in the direction Dex had gone with Tump. The creature's screams faded in the blackness of the night. I knew I would not get that lucky again. Luck and planning, not strength, had allowed me to win that battle. I knew when to quit. I had wounded the creature, but it would survive and learn from the experience. Another fight wouldn't be so easy.

I ran through the white sand, praying I wouldn't meet another creature like it. And I was also hoping for an early sunrise. I hoped Dex wasn't hurt too badly. I hadn't found any blood. Maybe his injuries looked worse than they actually were. I tried to find Dex's tracks, but there wasn't any sign of them. I kept moving in what I hoped was the right direction. The night was once again silent. The only sound to be heard was my breathing. I walked all night through the hot sand. At last the sun slowly rose. It was orange at first, then bright yellow. I once again stopped and watched the white sand turn pink, unbelievable as it was.

I started to walk again, taking my time. But I was getting worried; I thought that by now I would have found Dex and Tump, their tracks, or some sign that they had passed by here. I had been traveling in a zigzag fashion to cover more ground and, I hoped, find them. But so far there was no sign of either of them. My heart froze. What if Tump and Dex had been eaten by another creature? What if my plan had failed? What if there had been more than one creature out there last night? And if I had only lured one away, how could I live with myself? Well I wouldn't know for sure until I got to the oasis. The way that Dex was moving last night, nothing could have caught them. The Dark Ones weren't really that fast. They just surprised their prey by coming out of the sand at them. All that I could do was hope that Dex and Tump had made it.

It was noon. The sun was directly overhead. I was a walking zombie at this point. I hadn't had any sleep in a long time. Only a few hours on Dex's back, and that seemed like a distant memory. But I pressed on. I didn't want to spend another night out in the desert. I knew I was now on the Dark Ones' hit list. They would be looking for me tonight.

Up ahead a small mountain of boulders stretched as far as the eye could see. *Great*, I thought. As I approached it I saw that it wouldn't be that difficult to get over them. It was just a matter of hopping from one boulder to the next. So up I climbed, but jumping wasn't the problem. These rocks were hot! They burned my feet as I jumped from one to the other. I made it to the top in record time. Pain can make you move faster than you dreamed possible! The boulders were gray with a red tint. I was down on the other side looking back at the rocks. I sure didn't want to go back over them again.

The sun was now in my face, and I was running out of time. I had maybe three hours until sunset. As I scanned the desert, there was nothing in sight. I was in trouble. I sped up my pace. I was so tired and I knew that running was out of the question. I hadn't seen a single insect or other living thing since I had crossed the mountain of rocks. Only cactus, tumbleweeds, and thorn bushes.

Then I saw the holes in the sand everywhere. The desert looked like a piece of Swiss cheese. This must be where most of the Dark Ones slept. I was afraid that I'd never get out of here before dark. I somehow found the strength to run, leaping over the holes as I went. I ran through the desert for what seemed like hours, not slowing down. The sun was turning red and dropping below the horizon. I could feel movement beneath my feet. The Dark Ones were waking up, waiting for the last ray of sun to be gone. I could hear the creatures laughing and growling underneath me. The sun became a memory, and I was caught. My mind raced—there had to be a way out of this. But I could think of nothing, except to run. Ahead there was a tall cactus, at least twenty feet tall. I quickly climbed up to the top of the cactus. I was safe for a little while. I knew with their massive claws it wouldn't take them long to tear the cactus down. At least I would have a little time to rest and think.

Darkness blanketed the earth, the pink sand white and hot once again. Yellow eyes now appeared shining in the moonlight. They surrounded me instantly, growling and hissing.

"So," one of the creatures hissed, "you are the one who hurt our leader. Now we will even up the score."

Calmness came over me. I wasn't afraid. I'd much rather go out in a battle since there was honor in it. My worst fear had always been dying in my web and plopping on the ground with a splat.

I stared down at the Dark Ones and smiled. "Are you so sure you will win? There is more to me than meets the eye. I have traveled far, through the dark forest, over mountains. Through a swamp, and I have met and defeated many enemies. Do you think you can scare me? Pitiful creatures who hide from the sun don't scare me."

This made them pause, but only for a second. They knew that they had the advantage, since I was outnumbered. There were at least thirteen Dark Ones.

"Come down spider, come down and fight," the creature yelled.

"No," I said, "you come up here, if you dare. I'm waiting." I tried to sound fiercer than I actually was.

I pulled off four extremely long cactus needles and held them in front of me like a sword. The Dark Ones started leaping at my cactus, digging in with their long claws. But a few of them punctured themselves on the cactus needles. They fell down screaming; I couldn't stop laughing. Then I noticed that two of them were almost to the top. I was running out of time. The rest of them were clawing at the bottom of the cactus, trying to bring the whole thing down. I was constantly being knocked off balance by the vibration.

Everything was happening fast now, I couldn't stand up for very long. Every time I righted myself, down I would go again. Two creatures had reached the top and were coming toward me, but they were having trouble keeping their balance, too. They hissed at the others to stop, but they couldn't be heard. There was so much wild screaming going on, no one could hear anything being said. I had backed up and took a look down, to see if I had any room for escape. But I was surrounded. I thought that I saw a flash of light as I turned around to face my enemy. They were almost on top of me. I lunged forward and rammed the cactus needle I was holding into the creature's face. It screamed and backed off. I'm sure that it hurt, but it didn't do much damage. The second creature jumped forward and slashed at me. I didn't feel any pain, but suddenly I was off balance. As I fell on my side, I jabbed the cactus needle up toward it. I luckily caught the creature in the eye and it fell backwards. Why was I having such trouble standing, I thought dizzily. The first creature was heading my way once again. But something stopped it. It scrambled backwards, and down the cactus it went. I tried to get up again, and gave up. Something was wrong with me, but it was too dark to see. Where was that light coming from? I was alone on the cactus and it had stopped shaking. It was so silent, but the light was brighter than ever. I rolled over and looked across the desert. What I was seeing was unreal. A snake made of fire was weaving toward me. As it came closer I could see that it was actually a line of torches. It must be Dex's family. I waved and yelled and suddenly, there was Dex smiling at me.

"Hey, dude, sorry that we took so long to get here." I was being lifted down off the cactus. Once again I was on Dex's back. That's when it hit me. A wave of sickening pain ran through my body. Everything went black.

OASIS

Chapter Twenty-four

When I woke up, I thought I was still dreaming. I was lying under a big leafy tree on a soft pile of moss. The grass was brilliant green. There was a pool of aqua blue water with a hill behind it. A waterfall drained from the hill into the pond below. There were vines weighted down heavily with fruit. I was sure that I had died and gone on to my reward, but then I saw Tump's smiling face. He looked so worried and he had tears in his eyes.

"Hey, Tump," I said, "what's wrong with you, we're at the oasis now, aren't we?"

Dex walked over to me, and asked how I felt. I told him that my leg hurt, but other than that I felt all right. A troubled look washed over Dex's face. What was wrong with everyone? But I was too tired to talk and drifted back asleep.

The next morning when I woke up, Tump was still by my side. He smiled at me and again started to cry. I tried to sit up but for some reason I couldn't move. I looked down and saw my body was covered with wet yellow leaves. There were layers and layers of them covering me.

"What is going on, Tump? Why are you so sad, and why am I covered in these leaves?"

Tump opened his mouth to talk when Dex walked over to him and laid his hand on his shoulder. "Let me talk to him. Tump, you've been up all night. You need to go and get some rest now."

I was getting ready to yell at Dex, but I saw the sympathetic look on his face. I had a sinking feeling in my stomach. I was hurt worse than I had first thought.

"What is wrong with me, Dex?"

Dex took a deep breath, and said, "You fought so bravely last night. We have never seen anyone fight as fiercely as you did. But you have been injured, badly. One of those monsters clawed you, do you remember?"

"Yes, but it didn't hurt that bad, I remember that much," I answered him quickly.

"This is hard to say, Spinner, but you lost one leg and part of another on your left side. I'm sorry Spinner, there wasn't anything we could do."

I felt like all the air had been knocked out of me; this was impossible. I felt fine, and I could feel all my legs.

"You are lying to me Dex, I feel fine. Now get all these leaves off of me and I'll prove to you that I'm okay."

A very old, pale yellow lizard walked over and bent down next to me.

"Those are healing leaves, please, let them be."

"Who are you?" I had to know.

"My name is Istah, I am the healer. I'm sorry I couldn't do more for you. These leaves will help you heal quicker and keep the pain away."

She looked very old and wise. There was a gentleness to her that made me feel better. "I want to see for myself, please take off the leaves."

Slowly she removed layer after layer of the leaves. As she got to the last layer, my heart was hammering in my chest. She gently pulled it off, and I saw for myself. It was horrible. One of my left legs was gone. The leg next to it was just a stump. I couldn't stop the tears. With the leaves off, the air hit my wounds and the pain became unbearable. Istah saw what was happening and started to cover me up with the leaves. This gave me instant relief. I closed my eyes and tried to calm myself down. Crying would do no good. I had to find a way to live with this, but right now, I just wanted to feel sorry for myself. Tump and Dex tried to talk to me, but I stayed silent. How would I ever walk again? You are probably thinking, a spider has eight legs, what's one and a half less? But walking with eight legs is a precise balancing act. A complicated dance, where all eight partners must be in sync; when they were, it was poetry in motion. Now I would be a stumbling fool. Spinning a web would be close to impossible. My whole life had been altered drastically in a few seconds. All I wanted to do was sleep for a long, long time. So that is what I did.

At some point, Istah came to see me again. I tried to pretend I was asleep. She could tell that I was faking so she shook me until I opened my eyes.

"What do you want?" I growled.

"Don't you think that you have felt sorry for yourself long enough? There is much you still need to do. Your friend, Tump, is lost without you. He doesn't eat or sleep. He wanders around, trying to figure out a way to make things right for you again. Sometimes you have to look past your own problems, no matter how big they may seem. Tump will die without you, he is your responsibility whether you like it or not. So, let's get you well."

I looked at Istah, hating and loving her. She was right. I couldn't desert Tump. We still had a long way to go together.

"Will we be safe here for a while, Istah? There are others who want to hurt us," I asked.

"I know of the others, they can't come here. Just like the Dark Ones. This place is magical. No evil can enter. You are welcome to stay here for as long as you need to, forever if you like."

I thought about what she said and nodded in agreement. "You are right, Istah, but losing two legs is a little hard to deal with."

"I know young one," Istah said, "but you are gifted with extraordinary powers. I can help you use them to their full potential, if you would let me. You still need quite a while to recover and learn to walk again. Here you are safe and loved. I hope that you realize that. Young Dex told us how you sacrificed yourself, to give him and Tump time to get away from the Dark Ones. There are many who want to meet you, and will in time. But for now eat and rest."

"Thank you, Istah," I said with tears in my eyes.

Istah left and as I watched her walk away I saw Tump standing by the water.

"Tump, come over here and talk to me," I said.

Tump's eyes lit up and he ran over. He sat down beside me.

"How are you feeling now, Spinner?" he asked.

"I'm feeling a lot better, but you don't look so good, my friend. Haven't you been sleeping?" I asked.

"Oh, Spinner, I've been so worried about you. I just didn't know what to do. It's my fault that you got hurt; I feel so bad. You should have left me in the forest. I'm so sorry Spinner," Tump said through a stream of tears.

"Listen, Tump," I said carefully. "What happened wasn't anybody's fault, and I'm going to be fine. If I didn't want you to come along, I would not have taken you with me. You must know that. Tump, you are my best friend. We will always be together. We are family now. But if you don't quit blaming yourself, I will get mad. It looks like we are going to be here for a while. Is that okay with you? We are safe here from the Dark Ones and Miles. Besides, we both need to rest, and we have to decide what we are going to do. We can live here if we want. So for now let's enjoy our new home and get to know our new friends. I think we will learn a lot from them.

As I looked around, I thought, *This is like paradise.* I would recover and be stronger. I also knew our journey wasn't over. For now this magical place was our home, until the outside world allowed Tump and I to return to Witches' Brew Forest and our families once again.

The End